A Serenade's Form

This is the personal diary of Psychologist Alim Willem, and written within is the story of his struggle to detach moral discord from his therapy on a troubled young man.

SHAMSHER TARIQ

BLACK ROSE writing™

First printing

ISBN: 978-1-61296-944-2
PUBLISHED BY BLACK ROSE WRITING
www.blackrosewriting.com

Printed in the United States of America
Suggested Retail Price (SRP) $16.95

A Serenade's Form is printed in Adobe Garamond

This is the beginning of my literary journey,
and I am thankful to those who have found me here.

A Serenade's Form

Dear Victor,

You may find it strange to receive this letter so soon after your visit to me, but it was in fact seeing you that compelled me to do this. After all these years to still see your tears, tears for a story I have bound my heart to secrecy for, well, it was nothing short of my condemnation to write this to you. You see, I am too old now to care for shadows and masks. And time has belittled me too, for it does not forget. And so, I write. I suppose it is for the best, for my secret is heavy and no longer is hiding it a conditional chore.

Victor, tell me you knew. How could you have not? Though I suppose God is one for dramatics and so it is my ironic pen that spells the truth to you. I had not been fair to you, my friend. I had been dishonest, and in subtle ways and at certain times, monstrous too. And above all of this I have looked you in the eyes and smiled. Forgive this prose, my hands are trembling and my memories are blinding, too many of them. So because of it, I have sent with this my diary. In it is written the complete narrative of that little but detrimental moment of our lives. I myself haven't looked upon it since the day I forbade its content. But still, amusingly, its words ring in my ears like perverted drums; the consequence I celebrate. I surrender this to you, so that you may know the truth behind the facade of your friend.

13 August

For this certain case I have committed myself to this diary. I will keep it with me and every night before I sleep I will write in it the very peculiarities of the day, and a resume of my sessions with Alexander of that concerning day. As for now, the screeching of this train is driving me mad and I am writing to distract myself. I admit it feels almost liberating, and especially after years of writing patient reports and academic articles, to write leisurely of myself and of my friend, well, it certainly is of an appropriate practice for my return to Kazan, my first home. And I would be lying if I said I did not feel a brewing anticipation. It has been so long since I last set foot in this city and I wait to taste the familiar air, and as so, an odd nostalgia consumes me. Perhaps the bittersweet impatience I feel may be a subtle reminder of the love I still have for Victor.

When I last saw my friend we were both at the mercy of youth and it is only now can I smile in humiliation for the clumsy escapades we practiced. To even imagine then of what lay ahead of us would have been a strange thinking. But despite our strong belief in the euphoric condition, we matured and ultimately departed to pursue our interests. I struggled, for it was I who left the safety of familiarity and ventured into the ominous territory of possibility. Victor (although also very intellectually motivated), remained home in Kazan, and with this choice I wonder, as I have always wondered, did come for him the advantages of comfort? However so, he grew rich from exchange and since then has prospered elegantly. I still remember his letter inviting me to his wedding. He had married, as he said it, a "beautiful as wondrously bright" daughter of an established Conseiller of the Parisian system. I must remember to interrogate her on the matter of French law, and especially that of concerning the pathological; the pith of my wonder. Her name I believe is Fleur, and with her Victor bore his two children. He wrote about them too, often, and always, until the fading of his practice to do so. Why would, admittedly, one write to a ghost? I did not always find the time to reply, or perhaps it was motivation I lacked, for I did sometimes envy him. Perhaps I still do, for the memories of sitting in the rooms of my universities and imagining a life replicating the attractions of his, well, these memories still sustain an air of relevant emotion. Even now as I feel the threat of age, as I see the grey specs on my brow I wonder at what could have been. But I shouldn't complain, because despite the short comings of my luck and despite the cruel nature of my fortune, I too, once, touched happiness, and looked upon her with a look I yearn to feel again...yes...But ultimately, these superficial sensations must sometimes be ignored, for a man's oeuvre is his worth...it must be, for the sake of his sacrifice.

It is hard to believe a boy like Victor so full of dare and silly impulse grew to be a timid man content with the comforts of family life. I sincerely hope I can help Victor's son. It fills me with pride to know that Victor believes in my psychological research and practice. As of yet, not many intellectuals are convinced. It is a growing knowledge; vague are its theories, mysterious are its motives and vast is its study, and that is why I live a humble life. Poor Victor must be in a dreadful condition, for his writing was dour and terribly unlike the memory I have of him. Too many young men are drafted into this war. I must do my best to care for his son Alexander upon the boys return from post, which I was told should be tomorrow. The experiences of war can have the most disturbing effects on an innocent mind. Perhaps this visit would do me good as well. Ever since Agata's death I have felt incompetent towards my work. My patients have been dealt with poorly and it is most unfair to their desperate situations. I too, of course, have felt a strange loneliness, a yearning, and inexplicable sadness. An atmosphere of love and care will certainly invigorate my strength. I am nearing the destination! Perhaps I will write more later, after the formalities of settling in.

13 August (Later)

I am exhausted. The silence of my temporary bedroom is extraordinarily soothing, especially after today. What an emotional drain these past hours have been! I anticipated upon my arrival to the station a sentimental, yet casual reunion with my friend. But when I did arrive, waiting for me was one of Victor's chauffeurs, and of course, a luxurious Mercedes favored by the likes of kings. I was astonished…and vaguely embarrassed. All I brought for the family was Dostoevsky. What is more humiliating however, is the fact that when we were young it was I who confessed the passion for such luxuries. I know Victor would never flaunt his wealth, and his style of hospitality *is* unique, but is it wrong that I felt…mocked? Well, despite this sweet gesture of his, an ill part of me still wished to see on him the posture of exhaustion and the blemish of disappointment; I wished to see a man worn out by the coming of age, scarred with regrets. It's a funny thought, really. Perhaps it was me I wished to see. But Instead (and for the better), upon my arrival to the mansion I saw a different man. It was the colorful green and red attire of the ottoman culturist that attracted me first. The Caftan he wore swayed luminously in the sunlight as the big man hurried towards the car. Only under this stunning distraction did I notice the clumsy mannerisms of dear old Victor. As he stumbled towards me, I was tempted to fix my suede before stepping out to greet him. Immediately I was grabbed and pulled close to the giant man. When released, on his face I noticed the familiar smile I loved as a child, and I reflexively smiled back to him, full of a newfound joy and ridden of my malign anticipations. He hugged me again, kissed my cheeks and then practically carried me into his home. His enormous arms overwhelmed my shoulders, my God has Victor grown!

His wife and daughter are lovely, and I am sure his son Alexander shares this charm. Despite the anxiety this family faces for their beloved member, the atmosphere of this home is incredibly uplifting. I was smiling all through the night. Fleur Zaria really is intelligent and graced with exquisite exoticism. She is a creature devoted to the practice of education. Yet her poise *manner* of scientific discussion is what I admire. She not only understood perfectly, but interrogated further into every one of my introductions to psychological concepts. I was astonished, and oddly assuaged…Victor was dumfounded and looked on his wife with an amusing bewilderment. His daughter, Audrey Zaria is also very bright. She is only eighteen, a year younger than her brother, yet already she speaks with a tongue of aged scholars. Her knowledge and interest of world culture is admirable. In fact, she is so culturally inquisitive that Victor has hired a pianist for her. I am sure this is a form of distraction for the poor girl, who is overcome with worry but tries desperately to hide it. In her cheeks I notice a faint pallor common among my distraught. I am told this instructor will be joining us within the next few days. Pretty music flowing through the halls will be of great influence on all of our spirits. At dinner, Victor would not relent on praising my name. He complimented me arduously and told me how highly my name is regarded among the local universities. It is true I live a casual and an economically simple life, but of course I should take pride in how important and influential my work can be.

This day was wonderful, surprisingly. But even so I can't help but feel an occasional sadness. I miss Agata very much. She would have loved this trip and this family, and perhaps this atmosphere could have contributed to her the love I compromised in our marriage years ago… I am looking forward to meeting Alexander tomorrow, and in a few days' time we shall begin his therapy. No doubt he will have a lot to talk about and I am sure I can help him cope with the tragedies he has seen and experienced.

14 August

It was a quiet, calming day. In the morning I met the family at breakfast and we ate anxiously in wait for Alexander. Victor above all was transfixed with an excruciating trepidation. So in attempt to distract my solemn friend I confessed my desire to see the balcony and proposed to chat there with some of their foreign chai. Victor kindly agreed, but, unfortunately, used my proposal to excuse himself from the company and head upstairs. I kept the women in cheerful banter until a servant was sent calling for me.

I can't say for how long we spoke, perhaps a few hours in the least. It was a warm time and even at the balcony the breeze was fair. From Victor's first word I noticed a tremble in his voice. Never would I have expected *him* to surrender to emotion. Many times I watched his thick lashes soak with tears; he would then notice my staring and abruptly wipe them dry with his sleeve. I now feel the gravity of my responsibility. "Not a day goes by that I don't consider the reality of Alexander's situation, Alim." He said. "I know very well the odds of how quick my son could lose his life. Yet I continue the poor habit of hoping." The powerful, confident glare that is usual with Victor, now had a certain gleam of sentiment about it, and it humbled mine. I was at a loss for words, so I said nothing but tried comforting my friend with underwhelming gestures. "Don't think of me as selfish, friend. I know Agata's death hurt you too, and I don't mean to overwhelm you, never! But you see, Alim, I am *desperate*. Still, what you have taken upon yourself at this time, during your own tragedy, truly, it is a beautiful thing.

She was young, Agata, and from your letters, a wonderful person. The love you had for her, the poet you were! One would think you were majnun." My letters…is it cruel that I hardly remember writing them? He then got up and told me to wait a short minute as he disappeared into the room. A short minute later he rejoined me and held in his hands a tied bundle of paper. He passed it to me with a smile and spoke. "These are your letters, I had kept them and read them when had I missed you, dear friend. Now you should read them and laugh at the romantic you hide within your lettered name." I put on a smile as I took the letters from him, but it was a mysteriousness I felt towards them, the letters, for long gone are the feelings I once had upon the conjuring of them, and far away are the memories I once spoke so passionately of, as Victor attested. I think I murmured gratitude, and Victor took it as awe and nodded and settled back into his throne. I told him I would read them later as I surveyed them from front to back, but dared not to open and read in the presence of Victor; I could hardly but see the shadows of my enthusiastic script hiding within the aged covering.

Time passed in silence as Victor allowed me to roam within my mind for a short while, and then he spoke. "I want you to know that as long as you are here, you are a part of this family, you always were. It is unfortunate that we must reunite under these circumstances." It *is* unfortunate. Many times Victor invited me with open arms, he practically begged me to visit, so why *now*, I wonder. Could it be his humility towards me, his need for me? Is it self-gratification that brings me here? Or is it I who yearns for sane company? I am hoping I can understand this to be more than selfishness, but whatever it is, I must be fair with him, with his wife and daughter, but most importantly with his son, for the memory of Agata taunts me, the memory of my ignorance.

Victor grew anxious as the day passed and no word came about Alexander. I tried to distract him with other conversation, but to no avail. "He should be here by now." He would say to himself looking out onto the dimming roads. "I wonder what's keeping him." But eventually we both sat in quietness, hesitating to speak on a terrible wim, as above us seeped a darkening hue into the sky. I had closed my eyes inadvertently, and it was the grip of Victor's hand that woke me into a startle, and then I smiled as I looked onto the path of the front gate.

Oh how eager they were! We gathered and stood at the front of the home in a brilliant form to welcome the guest of honor. But as soon as the car neared, Audrey lost her patience and ran up towards it and frightened the driver into an abrupt stop; Victor laughed as Fleur shrieked after the happy girl and ran towards the car to hug her child. I took a subtle step back, perhaps naturally, but it was the right thing at the time, for it was a rather pleasant scene to behold as the stranger I felt I was.

The reunion was, despite the anticipation, rather calm; voices were mild and words were particular; behavior was formal and the embraces were somewhat quelled. I smiled, for this delicate atmosphere was the very gentle aura of happiness and liberating relief. And then I was introduced as Victor threw his son into my premature embrace, and spoiled my dramatic plans for a greeting. Alexander is a fragile thing. As I expected he shares the same lovely personality as his family. But physically he is dreadfully unintimidating; he is round at the face with golden hair on top combed perfectly like a child. He doesn't smile often, but occasionally one will notice the white pearls that are his teeth. He carries his mother's pretty, foreign eyes, her petite lips and centered nose too, but unfortunately, he also carries his father's form. After we spoke, after I heard his rosy voice, did I assure my belief that the battlefield could very likely be his grave and the state of war is a terrible one. "Alexander, this is Doctor Alim Willem." Victor couldn't resist adding in 'Doctor' every time he said my name, he must truly believe in my presence. "Alexa, he is here for you to talk to. There are things you would never tell your parents" he said this with a grin at me, obviously retreating to a time of youthful misadventure. "But this man, he is my greatest friend, and in being so has taken the responsibility of being yours as well." The boy seemed relieved upon hearing this but tried his best to hide it. I assured him that we would begin whenever he felt comfortable. And after that we sat down for dinner and heard but some of the exciting adventures Alexander experienced.

I have just read the first among the few letters Victor had saved from a time long gone. I can hardly believe that *I* wrote it, wrote them all, and no matter how hard I try to remember doing so, I just cannot seem to recall penning them. Though perhaps it is a good thing I have been given the chance to rediscover them. Not to mention, it will be amusing to see my growth and maturity through them…well, hopefully it is these qualities I see emerge from their expressions. I will copy-write the letters into this diary, both for the sake of preservation and to try and empathize with my younger self.

Hello Victor,

I have reached my university just fine. I am so pleased to see your letters waiting for me here, and it is nice to read the words of a dear friend after a long journey. I assume it is safe to say that our lives, after today, will forever more be different. I am looking forward to beginning my studies and finding my place as an intellectual. But my sweet friend, where would I be without you? Had you not held my dirty hand in the depths of poverty, I would be struggling as a dreamer. I promise to accomplish what I can, if not for myself, than for you and your family.

-Alim

18 August

These past days have been fairly calm. Alexander has become absolutely comfortable and is enjoying his temporary return. He seems to have an endless array of tales to share with us. His family is ecstatic to have him home, but Victor, within a stubborn masculinity, tempers his joy; I assume he wishes to remain an invulnerable force for his family during this time. I still wait for Alexander's confirmation to begin our sessions. Multiple times he has approached me hesitantly, always struggling to form proper words. But eventually he says something irrelevantly unimportant and walks away. The poor boy should not keep his thoughts to himself for much longer.

I was told that Audrey will begin her piano tutoring very soon. I have learned that the teacher is a young woman from the local town. She is recognized popularly in Kazan. Orphaned when young, and since then has lived alone I believe, at the town house for orphaned children; an experience I know well. Victor and I met in that neighborhood, by circumstance, we were young, wild and alike, a dangerous combination! And even considering the lavish fence between us, there is no partition, no politics, among children throwing stones at water. I don't know her name, but an artist's touch is their significance and so I am excited to hear her production. It will be good if Alexander feels a warm tension around her, perhaps it will distract him from his troubles. I too am excited to hear live music, for the recorders produce a most dissatisfying performance.

It is nearing midnight but I have no urge for sleep. Every time I close my eyes I hear that harmonious rhythm from earlier this afternoon. The tune still sings to me as I write this and I can't help but hum along to its memory. It was a fitting conclusion to the bittersweet journey of the day. It is mysterious to me now, as to how its sound spellbound me into a state of delirium; with care or maleficence? Is my musician a witch? But what did happen in the day? Well, I accompanied Victor and Alexander to the city in the morning and the trip was a strange delight, a satisfaction I believe I needed to feel for some unnoticed itch. I saw the same beautiful buildings as I had seen years ago, but now embroidered upon them were unique designs which are absent back home. Later I ate a delicious lunch of a foreign dish I cannot recall the name of. My two hosts showed me the area and took me to the new attractions that accumulate the tourists and admirers; this place has changed, as have its inhabitants.

And then we rode in a carriage through the more horrid of the neighborhoods; the ones forgotten by the appreciative eye and left to the care of poverty. And how familiar they were to me, every corner and every rugged brick, left in wait for me, and how anticlimactic was my return; a casual carriage ride through its broken yet heaving body. My return was not exactly how I had envisioned it; it was without the enamored robes and the golden airs, without the doves in the sky and the praises of my name from those I had left within the dirt. No, it was empty of everything pretty, but fulfilled by new faces of sadness, the familiar sadness that seemed to seep into generation from generation, a stubborn sadness that, like larva, fed off a uniformed body of life, or whatever it was that breathed this place alive. I felt uncomfortable through this tread sitting next to a bewildered Alexander as he most probably wondered upon the sins these souls had committed to be damned here. I wish I could have told him that there were no sins here, just men and women desperate to hold his hand, even for a minute; innocent lives looking up to him, as I did in my younger days. I wish I could have told him that not every one of these children would be as lucky as I was to be…rescued…by the likes of his father. *Rescued*? Do I dare write that? Well, isn't it true? Was it not my humoring of a rich child's playful nature that won me his heart? Were I poor *and* boring, would I have been noticed by the young, innocently selfish Victor? He chose me, like some toy to keep him company, and this above all provided me the opportunity to escape and grow as a proper man.

Had Victor even mentioned of our meeting to his family? Of course they know I belong to this neighborhood, they know I am an orphan, they know of my humble roots, but do they know of the humiliating circumstance their beloved husband and father found me in? Do they…pity me, or admire me? When I sit at the table with them, do they consider me, watch me? And what of the servants, do they belittle me within themselves, considering my belonging to a class below even them? Or am I simply paranoid, delusional and unfair to the hospitality of my friend and his family? But wait, I wonder if Victor himself even thinks of our meeting through my eyes, suspect what I truly feel surrounding our meeting; my feelings. No, he is ignorant, completely, and his interrupting of my wild thoughts with his speaking was an exact proof of it.

He spoke so fondly of the memories, and so poignantly too in fact, that he had had them seem like dreams. As we rode along I watched him smile heartedly at the passers and the confused but awed children looking up at us. Victor had a strange grin, a grin of sympathy and what I assumed to be pity, but I could be wrong, though I doubt I am. He told us both of the history of this place, as if I didn't know it myself, and as if Alexander was a tourist among a land of plague. He began to point out irrelevant businesses and establishments, ones that should have no importance to him or anyone, but only to those who survive off of them. I looked ahead and tried to see the coming roads, hoping to soon leave this neighborhood; why did I feel so condescended? Not once did Victor mention the poverty of the place, but I could sense it within his words and his gaze, and from his son's look of shock. But I was silent and rode along by their sides pretending to be absolved within the sights.

And then it came, upon a hill connected to society by a single withered path of stone, the orphanage. That building, it had been years since I had seen it, and how appropriate of its nature to have changed nothing since my escape from it; I expected nothing less. I said nothing, naturally, for what is the purpose of my recollecting it? And so we rode near it and nearly passed it with not a nod for it, but Victor and his sweet obliviousness, to particularly point it out to me and the boy and ask me with a brutish grin, whether or not I remembered it. I did, and I managed to smile upon my confirming of his rhetorical question. He told Alexander of how there is a lake behind it, and in the afternoons of his childhood, he would sneak away from his home and come to me, specifically, so we could play at the lake. And as he spoke I too began to remember the sweet memories of our throwing stones into the waters, and running and swimming, and nearly drowning....and laughing. I managed to wipe my eye without alarming the two beside me. It occurs to me now, perhaps too late, but regardless, it occurs to me that these memories, this place is not the same poverty stricken land to Victor as it is to me; perhaps this place is a refuge for him, his most endearing memory, and because of me…but, I cannot be fooled by sentiment, how can one look upon this place with endearment, and especially one among the likes of Victor? No, these emotions are a facade of a truth, of a reality, of my reality, and nothing more. But still I love him, this, I cannot deny.

We returned to the home during high noon and I was worn out. I said hello to Fleur and to the servants and then retired to my room, hoping not to have to greet any other. Silence immediately spread all around as I closed my door and lay on my bed.

The exhaustion that burdened me began to embower me, so I closed my eyes. But it was then as I lay in bed waiting for the comfort of sleep, that the soft tune began to play and echo all around. Audrey and the instructor must have begun their musical lesson. Audrey is just learning, so this tune must have been the work of her teacher. It was a unique theme, one I hadn't physically heard before, but one I understood at its immediate sound, a sound I recognized, a sound I empathized with. And especially after the re-exploration of my childhood earlier in the day, I felt a certain comfort in its conduction, as if I was home, amidst familiarity and family. The player knew me, or parts of me, parts unknown to the outside world, and each note was a little secret. At first I was conscious and captivated, but slowly I felt each note of the chopinesque theme dap me with fatigue and eventually did I fall, peacefully, into sleep. I must remember to compliment her when we meet. Unfortunately, I have slept through dinner! That is all I have to write for now. I will sit here quietly on my bed like a fool and wait for the sweet satisfaction of sleep.

Victor,

I am so glad to hear of your externship. Was there ever a doubt? And me? Well, I would say things are fine, nothing too extraordinarily interesting here, other than the bitter colds. Actually, do you remember the polish baker, Svysten? Well, I do not mean to shock you, but I have found another man with a thicker accent than his. Yes! It's true! He is my professor, so you must pray for my results. Though his sweet daughter accompanies him occasionally and manages to translate some of his demanding directions for us. She is a student herself, and now that I think about it, seems a bit too invested in the books of Rumi and the dramatist Shakespeare, can you believe it, in this day and age? Perhaps I should speak with her, to see what it is that consumes her. Now, now, before you accuse me of anything, I am simply bored with the constant academic atmosphere, and need a leisurely conversation with a sane person. And well, she provides this opportunity. How are your parents, Victor? I have been missing them. Are they still so adamant on finding you a wife? Let me tell you, run away to France for a weekend, they cannot reach you there, and I hardly doubt they want to! I look forward to hearing from you, my friend.

-Alim

24 August

I feel strange. Today's experience has me under a curious charm. I am still smiling like a man virgin to love. I can't remember when I last felt a feeling this sweet, yet ironically terrifying. Despite my spirit, I will try not to exaggerate the eloquence of today's ambiance, but here is what happened: I woke at noon. The ripe sunlight was lulling. The shutters were open, so through the rooms and through the halls there spread a sweet but gentle lily scented draft; its air was clean and satisfying and it impressed my thirst for more. I lay awake there and savored in the safety of the morning breath. Needless to say, I was well rested and of elated spirit. Through the silence of my room intruded an obscure hymn, it was Audrey's.

Her canorous sound only but adorned the pretty air. Soon it vanished and the ticking of my watch reminded me of the time and prompted me into appropriate dress. I left for the dining room in hopes of catching at least one member to dine with. But as I passed the library I discovered Victor, Fleur and Alexander sitting there in leisure, discussing what I assume to be the details of the ball Victor intends to throw within the coming weeks. Victor noticed me through the thick air of his cigar and brushed through it towards me, and after my apologies he urged for me to go down and eat. I obeyed eagerly and left them. I reached the piano room and the familiar hymn sang again, Audrey's inspiring presence was touching. She was ignorant of me as I watched her ready the seating for her piano lesson. I thought of the instructor and an odd curiosity overcame me. I decided to leave Audrey continue her chore undisturbed; I set off again to satisfy my growing hunger. I was now on the first floor and headed towards the dining room. Walking towards me was Kurya, the butler, and following him was a woman I hadn't seen before.

My hunger was demanding, so I gave a little smile to the man and continued walking, considerably distracted. As I passed the woman however, a jasmine-scented air touched me. It aroused my senses and drowned my hunger. My pace dulled as I breathed in the lustrous breeze of the stranger's stroll, it was...enlivening. I was however, brought back into sensation by her voice, for I had just heard her call *my* name. I wondered, and so for a moment I stood there perplexed, and it was, certainly, warmer than before. I confess I cannot exactly describe the pretty melody of her sound or the interesting rhythm of her accent, but I will say that my attraction for it is a hauntingly familiar feeling I have become almost ignorant of.

"Dr. Willem?" She repeated; I was now, of course, certain, and so I turned to face her. She stood with a humble composure yet there was, ironically, a mark of wonder on *her* countenance. She is young, not much older than Audrey. Foreign features design her face and her grin does carry this odd crook, but otherwise she is interesting to the eye. I obeyed her invitation and approached her.

"Good morning" I said reaching out my hand. "Forgive me but I don't exactly recognize you." She grasped my hand and I could swear to have felt a blush swim through my cheeks.

"I don't expect you to, Doctor." Her eyes surveyed me and her odd grin was gleaming…clearly I had her attention. The soft touch of her hand was a unique one, and immediately she became, interestingly enough, familiar.

"Oh, you must be Audrey's instructor." I said, and to which she nodded quite curiously. I continued speaking without even giving her the chance to accept the honor. "Well, you're very talented. I heard you playing with Audrey. It was beautiful playing, very…but of course a note or two were a bit misused but, what do I know about music, it was nice regardless and…easily put me to sleep." I soon came to realize that my latest compliment hardly sounded like one, and I stuttered, the woman smiled, and Kurya coughed.

Of course she wasted no time in exploiting me. "Well I hope not, Doctor. That's not what every musician likes to hear."

"Well I don't see why, sleep is an important thing." I said, trying desperately to save my dignity. "But may I ask, how do you know *me,* miss…?"

"Isabelle Vera, Doctor. And any enthusiast of science would know your name. Your research on the unstable is an interesting one. Really, to survive the consequences of crawling through their minds takes an incredible capability."

"Yes…" Survival? That is an interesting thought. "Well, I hope I did survive, Ms. Vera. Thank you." Her glare became intimidating and I could hardly look her directly in the eyes, for every time I did, my heart skipped.

"I can't believe you are actually here. I know it's for Alexander, Audrey told me, but still I would love to learn more about your work."

"Of course"

"Thank you, I should get going. Audrey will be waiting for me and I don't want to be let go! I hope to see you soon." I stood there, still, watching her walk up the steps until she disappeared around the corner. Kurya must have noticed me, for he interrupted my day dreaming with ridicule.

"Hungry, Sir?"

For the next two hours I was in full concentration to the music playing above me, but especially to its producer; For the rest of the day I was lost in thought, and because so I gave miserable attention to everything around me. Alexander even approached me, but even though he once again failed to accomplish valid conversation, I felt annoyed by his interruption. I felt a sudden irritation by his indecisive behavior, by his meek hesitation. That is why I should not let this mysterious infatuation interfere with my responsibilities and priorities. Now I should try to sleep, hopefully it will come soon.

Dear Victor!

Is not the wandering Aengus within me? If I could, through the fortunes of imagination, translate to you the feelings in my heart, well would you not wonder if I was majnun! But I am not a poet, but a madman, in love, and well, is there much a difference then? Sometimes in the day I forget my purpose here, my strivings, for I glimpse her and a happiness screams through me, an emotion I hadn't known to have existed outside the fiction of the Greeks. Her name is Agata, and I am somewhat certain, that she just might probably be, infatuated with me as well, and well, I will keep you in touch with my endeavor.

Goodbye, dear friend, Alim

26 August

I found Isabelle waiting for Audrey today, alone in the library by the piano and admiring the works of art showcased; both the literary and visual displays. I decided to interrupt her, for a question had bothered me for some time before this, and was there a more perfect opportunity? I said hello and she did too and I asked her to sit with me a while as we waited for Audrey. And then we spoke, on this and that, on colors and music, and language too, on her name and her history. I told her I too was raised in the orphanage by the hill in which she lived all her life. She smiled and said she knew, and asked me my secret to escape. To this I laughed a sad little laugh, for it truly was escape. Not from the people, no they were lovely, as Isabelle agreed. But it was the state of stagnancy, the hopelessness that followed me until my departure from it. I told her this, and she surprised me with her reply. She said that this was the very reason for her stay, that certain guilt would besiege her were she to leave the others, the children; I sighed to myself.

I told her there would always be children there, and asked her if the opportunity came for her to leave, what would she do? She smirked and said she would confront the possibility then, and until then will play her music; a modern muse she is.

I do see a longing behind her eyes, an unsettled dream of accomplishment. I changed the topic to her music and asked her where she had learned to play. To my much admiration, she had taught herself with the observance of the musical guests at the orphanages, and ultimately with her practicing on the choir piano that was hardly ever used. Yes I remembered that piano. I told her it was a gift to an ill caretaker of ours, and when she had passed had left the piano untouched and unheard for the coming years. I then thanked her for bringing a pretty sound into the place, and I was reminded of the familiarity I felt through her playing with Audrey on her first lesson, and I smiled. This was to the curiosity of Isabelle who questioned me on it. I felt comfort overcoming me with her every voice and I did not want to speak but stare at her with a sense of relief; she was confused but amused, and was about to question me again, but Audrey came in apologizing for her tardiness. I welcomed the girl, said goodbye to them both and left. She is an interesting girl, Isabelle, and I am glad I have met her. I feel a little more at home with her here; a little peace to my trembling, a calming to my growing fear of this something, a something that I haven't felt until very recently.

29 August

She came again today, as is her duty. I found myself waiting eagerly through all the morning to see her, as would a child. I had grabbed the chance to watch them play. But there was something interesting about Isabelle that preoccupied me. It was a certain passion, a certain heart, one she embodied with an authenticity, with a respect unfounded until now. Her state was of a musician's style, femininity was of other concern. Yes, her expression was in-consideration of her oeuvre and nothing more. Her belle tied hair was simply an artist's leisure, as were the clipped nails of a pianist's hand that she wore so proudly, or, blissfully? Even the confident spine she controlled was, I assume, a product of her method. She was modest though, undeniably so. For the music she produced was of good nature complementing moral and chaste. But still she was un-superficial with the self. She was honest, real, human…and so I fell.

1 September

Alexander has been avoiding me. I fear he has surrendered all courage to approach me or to even speak to me about what happened. Victor has noticed this and is most disappointed. He urges me to speak to Alexander, so I have tried but with no success. The boy continues to advert the subject. He is in no way unkind to me or disrespectful in any way. In fact I think he admires me, maybe even envies me. Sometimes I catch him replicating my posture; He speaks to me only of my literature and admires how I "keep to myself." But he avoids any subject related to his experiences or the war in general, so I won't push him or encourage him to speak. I throw subtle hints about the important topics, and he cleverly escapes with quick aversion. I must respect his decision and retire this therapeutic regime. I will tell Victor about this soon. Perhaps it is of no use after all, the boy seems more than happy with the company of his family and friends. He has taken a liking to Ms. Vera. They seem to get along quite well and share a wonderful liking for piano. It bothers me a bit seeing her so kind to him, but this mediocre jealousy is dangerous and will only hurt my treatment towards Alexander, so I will try to think of other things.

My own relationship with Ms. Vera is blossoming. We seem to have a lot in common. She seems delighted with my company, and I with her, obvious to me by now. I meet her when she visits and she refuses to leave until bidding me goodbye. Although she knows of my situation and the death of dear Agata, she avoids any confrontation to the subject. I too am hesitant to speak of it just yet. For now I will keep this mellow pace and let time tell.

The ball was a beautiful time, with colors and music and scents I hadn't experienced since mine and Victors graduation; his parents had presented it as a gift to us both, but we were clever then, and had discovered the secret reason for its grand preparations; Victors parents were quite enthusiastic to find him a wife to say in the least. But nonetheless we allowed it, or I should say celebrated it, for who doesn't love the company of lovely young women to dance with every now and then? But of course Victor's parents were rather disappointed with the result of it, seeing me by their son's side by the end, even despite their efforts! Though this disappointment only lasted a year or two, until the day they were introduced to a remarkable girl from Paris.

And today's ball was a pretty little memory that reminded me of the dear times of my innocence. I had danced with the beautiful women of the house, and drank fresh wines conjured through the stripping of the vines and the enamorings of alcohol. I wore the clothes of a romantic man, among the likes of the Zaria men, and I humored the passionate ballet that strung my feet into a dance, and that, not by chance. But I was sad, at times, noticing no one but her, the girl, as I longed to hold her hands and sway onto the stage amidst the flowery air, with her swaying hair. I am not sure why, for I hardly know her, but I was so tempted by her presence, and so eager to demonstrate it too. But I was also reluctant, for I couldn't detract the attention and the minds of those present by accompanying Isabelle through it all. So I waited for an appropriately subtle moment, and grabbed her hand at the sound of Chopin's *Berceuse*, a mellow peace intended for a simple transition of mood, but it is lovely, and so, I took advantage of its beautiful quality. Her eyes grew as I led her through, and I noticed a peeking smile through her subtle style, as I walked her down the pleasant aisle. She commented on the orchestrated adaption of the piano masterpiece, and I agreed obliviously, for I know nothing. She laughed at it, my confident ignorance, and I did too, warming the space between us. And with what coincidence did the melody shift into another, more romantic theme of, well, Chopin's *Romance*.

We were practically alone in the center, with the exception of Maxim and an unnamed maiden, and Alexander and Audrey, and soon following was Victor with Fleur. I felt more comfortable with Isabelle after the joining of the other members; certain privacy overcame us as the attention of all was stolen by the enamored host. I was absolved within our trance and assumed her to be so also, for how long-fully she held my arms with her musical fingers tenderly pressing me and quivering through my skin and bones, and dabbling upon my heart; her spellbinding method. But this was perhaps in my delusion? I enjoyed it, whether it be in my delusion or not, for never would I be given another chance, I believe. And rightfully so, for soon came the plea of Alexander to steal her away from me.

I gave her up and she let go. But through this delusion of mine I swear to have felt a hesitancy in her doing so, and If not by her hands, then by the glancing look she gave upon the turning of her strands. I then walked back to the sides and watched a growing population dance to the coming waltzes, and tried, to my greatest failures, to unnotice the duo of my envy. Audrey came to me and we spoke on some of the clothing's and the foods, and some of the very strange looking guests too, and then I asked her to dance, for every woman her age deserves this at least thrice within a ball. She accepted within a thrill and pulled me onto the center and led me and criticized my rhythm too, and I nearly regretted my chivalrous invitation. But how lucky of me to be saved by an unlucky man who came and asked for her hand, and how cute was his confident smile as he took to stand. Then came fleur and I danced with her, and from her I drifted into the arms of another, and from there to somewhere, and then back to Fleur, and unfortunately to Audrey too, whom I slightly swung onto her brother, and then drifted into the crowd, only to be met with Isabelle's shroud. I held her and she held me, but upon our first step came a thunderous breeze, and within a second past held in my arms was the giant Victor. He had a gleaming smile and swung me from side to side as the others laughed. He yelled something about our younger days as we danced to my sweet humiliation.

The ball ended an hour past this moment as the moon struck its peak. It took quite some time for the crowd to dissipate and until I was given the chance to retire to my room and bid all goodbye; though I missed out on finding Isabelle departure. I wonder about her feelings after today, and what she had thought about our little moment together; it was a random thing, an impulse I had acted upon without a second thinking towards it, but it was strangely important, at least to me and to the satisfying of my curiosity for the girl. But even despite her, the ball was a brilliant time and I could never thank the family enough for allowing me the chance to experience something like this again, and for reminding me of my romantic self and awakening a certain fun within me. Goodnight.

12 September

As I expected, I have been dreadfully unprofessional. I am treading close to the ethical boundaries of my profession. I am letting my emotional sensitivities get the best of me. Here is what happened: Yesterday morning as the Zaria family and I sat down for breakfast, Alexander was handed a letter. This note was Alexa's call to his post; he is due to leave us in two days. So all day yesterday and for the most part of today, Alexander as well as the family had been under a most upsetting sorrow. Audrey had tried her best to keep their spirits high, but to little effect. What is strange though is that I felt as a complete stranger to this atmosphere. Amusingly, I had *tried* to feel as dispirited as the rest but the thought of Isabelle kept me disassociated, or it did at least until this afternoon, to which I then adopted a delusion. Today she visited at her daily time and noticed the distress grimaced on each member of the family. She encouraged Audrey to play and would not relent on expressing her pretty gestures to all those around. Eventually she succeeded in gathering us all into the library and implored Alexander to join her at the seat. As I sat next to Victor indifferently, I watched Isabelle hold Alexander's hand so tenderly and lead him to the piano seat; a hot feeling then swam through me. Now that I think about it, today Isabelle had completely abandoned her formalities towards me; she hardly noticed I was there. Instead she smiled heartedly at and flirted with Alexander. Well not romantically, but she was all too friendly, wasn't she? But it *was* of appropriate behavior in attempt to extinguish his sadness; still, I could not help but feel a bit teased. Alexander too seemed assuaged by this touch and immediately succumbed to her desire.

I watched them share a smile as they settled next to one another on the piano seat. Her hair brushed his arm with a certain delicacy, a happening obvious to only me. And they laughed, to my envy, as a mutter whispered from her lips, to no one but the boy. Victor was interested by the duo, and was considering their secret nature, as I. Victor noticed my trembling hands and asked me if I was feeling alright. I turned to him lazily, thought of a mediocre lie and was about to say it too, But it was then, almost immediately, capturing our entire sensitivities, did Shubert's Serenade render into the air.

It was the type of sound that grabs your soul and strengthens its grip with every perfect touch of the keys. Every note tingled in my bones and carried me powerfully through the poignant beauty of the serenades form. A wonderful sensation burned through the hairs on my skin. But at the same time, for some odd reason, I was...*enraged.* The audience adorned the playing with unconscious awe, of course. But I, *with absolute confliction,* expressed an indifferent visage. Their fingers, Isabelle's and the boy's occasionally touched, and with every touch I felt weaker and sick and miserable. I stood up despondently, but furtively, and moved myself to the chair in the back, isolate and hindered. Victor watched me with weary eyes, though he was inattentive and considerably exhausted with sentiment, and therefore unaware of me. I too, in attempt to calm my nerves burned a cigar and breathed in its warmth. My head fell back as I watched my smoke rise above me and move in the air to Shubert's melancholic ingenuity, and to the duo's tender demonstration of it. They too, the audience, began to glisten with joy as the music induced in them a calming. I, isolate and vestige, was inhibited by the agitating aestheticism of the sound.

After the music faded to an end and the atmosphere slowly dulled the fidgeting began. I however, remained seated; my eyes fixed onto Alexa's stupid smile and immediately, almost frighteningly, my blood seethed with fiery. Did I *want* to hurt him? I don't think so, but I did want him to leave, to just disappear. And I wanted him to see me too. I was I believe in a sort of capture upon the boy, for neither could the oscuro slowly burning through my fingers, nor the pulsing rhythm of my beating heart bring me back to sensation, but rather, it was Victor's potent hand touching my shoulder that did. To which I stood, with nervous immediacy, to his attention. We exchanged some trivial comments about the music and about his son's hidden musical talent, and then he left the room and following him was Fleur, I nodded to her as she hardly noticed me while in her stupor.

I turned back to the boy and saw that Audrey had joined

his company. The siblings walked with Isabelle towards the doors side to side, still subdued in musical, ecstatic conversation. It then dawned onto me a terrible dare. Without thinking, I crushed the smoke onto a tray and walked hesitantly to the trio. I interrupted them by placing my hand on the boy's shoulder and indicating my desire to speak with him. Staring into his eyes I asked him if I could steal a moment of his life, there then formed a unique form of modesty in his eyes as he looked inquisitively into mine…or perhaps, I wonder, if it was fear I saw. He did oblige obediently and then thanked Isabelle farewell. I too nodded to her as she left with Audrey arm in arm. But before she disappeared completely I saw her throw a glance at us both, I wish I could have understood it.

With Alexa waiting patiently behind me, I closed the doors of the room and then turned around to face him. An uncomfortable quietness spread around the room as the last echo of the piano died. Sweat gathered on my palms, but a terrifying empowerment did overcome me. I walked to him directly and asked him to one of two single sofas placed in front of the scenic window. He settled into one and began to stare pensively out into the fields. "Did you like the music, Doctor?" he asked, despaired. I sat on the sofa across from him and said I did. But I told him it was time we began our sessions and this childish avoidance of the fact was a waste of time for us both. I believe he overlooked the imprudence of my remark for he simply laughed nervously in agreement, but still looked outside; his eyes feared to face my own. I knew very well that this situation was an abomination to the idea of counseling, yet I continued it on with a disgusting confidence.

"Alexander," I said. "How are you feeling?" He sighed.

"I'm Alright, and yourself? Did you like the music? Isabelle's incredible, did you notice? She even made me sound alright!" I could feel his heart stutter at the very sound of his rendering Isabelle.

"Alexa, we really should talk about you, and not of Isabelle, and not of music; you're being sent back to the war. And about the post this morning, you must have noticed the distress it caused your family after you read it *aloud?*" He shook his head as his eyes began to glisten and his nose began to flutter. Oh how I hate myself! Why couldn't I control my tongue?

"Ah, you're right, Doctor!" he exclaimed. "I see it in their eyes. They have no faith in me. They see me and probably wonder how long I will survive. You know, Doctor, I am not a soldier, I will die. It is just a matter of when. I wait for it, expect it."

"Yes, well it's hard to come to terms with the fact that you will die. But at least you can say you died for your country, died for your family, yes?"

He scoffed. "Country, what an honor! No, Doctor. Nationalism is the death of free thought. I am fighting for just a name, for pride of the beasts who control us. They send us with guns and blades onto battlefields to kill other men like us. I see my own face on every single boy I murder. But I do it for a cause, yes? For my country. Just as they die for theirs. And family, well I suppose dying is the only way I can support them then, Doctor?" He said, a laugh croaked in his throat. I wanted to say yes, to break him down. But he continued. "You must know how it feels, to see nothing in your parent's eyes but fear when they look at you?"

"My parents are dead, Alexa." It was not the guilt I wanted that peeked through his eyes upon hearing this, but rather, it was pity, and I felt belittled, as I always have for superficial reasons in this house. It was at this moment I realized my considerable hate for Victor's son. My voice spoke with a sudden intensity, a sort that made *me* dread it. "I'm curious, Alexa, how is it on the battlefield? It must be a thrilling experience, yes? I hear when one approaches death, they think a lot of God, of heaven and hell, yes? Is that true, Alexander? What do *you* think about?"

He crossed his hands, he trembled and his eyes watered. For a moment he froze too, until opening his lips to speak. I waited with crippling anticipation. And then he whispered, "I think, Doctor, of death, yes, of blood too. Did you know it's much darker, the color of it I mean, when you see so much of it. It's thick and smells like...*iron*. To think of that in my body, it's interesting. To feel it swimming through my veins with such pressure. But I also think of Audrey and my parents. I dream too! Dream of walking through bodies and falling face to face with my own, and I, *cry*. And then I think of heaven. I wonder, Doctor, how can one be happy in heaven without imperfection? Do you understand? I wonder, when I remember my childhood, for example, I smile, yes? The childhood memories that make me love those around me; the ones who created my memories, the memories that have me admire the frailties of youth. So, Doctor, how can one be happy in a white world without the nostalgia or the people that makes them appreciate, well, living? What is this happiness that we are promised? Is it materialistic, shallow happiness? How can we be happy if our fathers or our sisters burn in hell? Does God take away our feelings? Our sympathy? If so, what then makes heaven so great? Without the concern and fear of danger and of sorrow, without the acknowledgement of deprivation, how can we really appreciate the happiness we are experiencing in Heaven, it is forced onto us! If I have no curiosity, no want, then of course I will be satisfied with what I am given, even if it is nothing, yes? We are blinded in Heaven by this veil of splendor, are we not?"

I was, obviously, at a loss for words, but interestingly moved by his lunacy; I was interested to hear more. "Forgive me, Doctor...Actually, I just realized, I love Isabelle." I should have stopped him there, it was the better thing to do. "Listen, Doctor. How can I be happy in this *paradise* if she doesn't love me? How can I be happy if she too lives in heaven, but with someone else, someone *she* loves? If God lets me be with her, then how is it fair to her? Is she forced to love me too? Or is my love for her taken away so she can be happy? And if that's the case, then what a cheat God is! Help me understand, Doctor, please. How can I truly be happy if someone else comforts her? You know Doctor, if the love of Heaven Is one that hides my need for Isabelle, then that is a love I don't want.

In fact, it makes me wonder, what can I do to impress her? I have already committed myself to learning well the intricates of music; do you think that would impress her? Will she love me, Doctor? Do you know? Can you imagine how I feel? To be mad for her? I think I will tell her how I feel now, before I die, I must, yes?" He turned to me confused, his eyes red and pupils frantic.

"I think, Alexa, you need to calm yourself and think. Do not involve her into your misfortune, your death. Let her live and be. If you truly love her, then drop this stupid idea. You don't even know if you will go to heaven or hell. You don't even know if this promise is real, so why think so dramatically about it? We could die and be forgotten by God, by his angels too…and never even know what Isabelle thinks of us, do *you* understand? And you are being selfish; your death affects your family the most, so think of them! Stupid boy, understand this! Death is a part of life, and yours could be, is, very soon. Accept it, yes?" The sun was setting and he wept like a madman upon its majesty. "You speak of impressing Isabelle. My dear boy, what can you do? Are you a scholar? Are you even a *student?* You're a soldier, fighting for a country you don't even love, there is no passion in your heart for what you *can* do, so tell me then, what is there for Isabelle to love? No, my dear boy, forget about Isabelle. Women love the mind and the knowledge it yearns for, and they love our passion for it. You can *commit* to learning all of music, all of science, you can boast your love for it all, you can hide yourself behind automobiles and mansions, but what you *know now,* that is what defines you." I don't deny in seeing the insult to victor. Alexa had his face buried in his hands. "Either way, whatever she may feel, whatever she may think, she can't love a dead man, Alexa." A deadening pause spread. My voice was monotonous, baleful. "Look at me, Alexander."

But he avoided me. I intimidate him and the poor boy doesn't even know. I am still in shock, despite what I may feel. Never have I been so careless, so personal with my care. I felt it appropriate to end the session there, so I stood up and walked over to him and placed a hand on his shoulder, one that I felt tremble within his bones. "Well I think that's enough for now" I said. And then I left him, my nephew, my friend, sobbing on the sofa. On my way out I heard him say this: "Thank you, Doctor." I said nothing back to him.

Is this love? If so, then what form of disgusting love is this? A love rooted in jealousy and hatred, no, this is not the love I want. I don't think I could forgive myself if something did happen to him. His words do touch me; in fact they invoke in me a sudden wonder. I can't help but think of the humiliation I will feel when facing Victor and Fleur tomorrow, and for a reason I cannot even understand. Alexander is a delicate child, he is loving and faithful, and so, can I trust myself with him? I must be careful or I will break him.

14 September

The past two days seemed to have recovered the mood from before the duet. The house seems much too vacant now. Occasionally I am met with a friendly smile; otherwise I only hear the sounds of tension. With just the looks of the eyes this family has the most intricate of conversations. I myself have a hard time keeping the family sensible, for they refuse to accept the truth of poor Alexander. Since Alexander left this morning, not one person has uttered a single acknowledgeable word. All day yesterday however, Victor and Fleur would argue about their son's behavior. Alexander did not show himself until his departure. Victor would keep knocking loudly on his door but was only answered with silence. I wonder whether this situation could be of my doing, because of what I had said to the boy. But I should not assume, Alexander is much too sentimental.

This morning he left early enough to avoid confrontation with his family. I woke to the sound of Victor shouting his sons name and stumbling down the front steps of the home. In my daze I rushed to find some robes and follow them downstairs and approached the noise. I was led to the front of the house and there I saw the dramatic scene. Audrey was following after her mother, who was in effect running after Victor. Victor, in his haste and shaken nerve, slipped and lay prone on the cement path moaning Alexander's name as his sons car drove away from us and disappeared into the far away mist of the dawn. Transfixed, I waited at the front door for the bare foot family to gather the strength and the self-respect needed to face the servants and me. After standing up her father with the help of Fleur, Audrey ran up to me and embraced *me* tightly. It was strange to me, I would've never thought of myself to be so close to her to, but I tried my best to comfort the poor girl and held her back. Victor was limping as Fleur gently helped him walk, I let go of Audrey and ran up to help my friend the rest of the way into his home; he had hurt his ankle during the fall and has been in bed all day today.

I sat with them in the library soon after. Fleur was a quiet hysteric as she cried into her hands and brushed off Audrey's attempted embraces. Victor lay on the sofa nearby and stared mysteriously into the ceiling, tears unfit for his size dripped down his cheek. I brought them tea and said some underwhelming condolences. I then advised Audrey to take her father up to his room; he must now be bedridden due to his sprain. The two left, so now I remained alone with a still Fleur. I kept my hand holding hers softly. She did not speak at all but rather stared pensively, like Alexander did, through a rather interesting window. She then herself let go of my hand and walked out of the room without muttering a single sound. As for myself, I first advised Kurya to remain aware but calm, to answer attentively to their calls and to keep a close eye on them all. I then shut myself into my room and slept for another good hour. I woke to a high sun and a warm air. As noted, the halls were rather empty and abandoned, for the servants are themselves quite confused and weary in wake of this event. I strolled through the vacancy and admittedly, and quite shamefully, savored the sudden silence. As I ate breakfast alone in the dining room, a somewhat worried young servant came to me and said that Victor wished to see me when I was ready for him. I dismissed him and finished the meal in leisure.

Victor is in grave condition, he is pale and worn out. He smells of sweat and tears; this is not the Victor I remember. I couldn't say much to him except "Alexander will be fine" or "get some rest, friend." But interestingly he felt much better with just my company. He continuously took responsibility for Alexander's odd departure. He spoke to me of how he pushed dear Alexander too hard. It is upsetting to know just how aware Victor is of Alexander's fragile personality. I then eventually advised my friend some rest and promised him my return. As I left he told me to stay in his home for as long as I wished and of how important I have been for his family. What could have been my answer? Is it wrong that it was Isabelle rather than the family I thought of to spend my prolonged time with? The rest of the day as noted was rather slow, quiet and dull. Audrey shut herself away in her room and would not answer even to her personal girl. I am ashamed to say that Fleur could have done well to do the same. I sat with her again for a while in the library, but this time it was odd, because she spoke very often, but not very concisely, and as she spoke she sewed inattentively. She told me stories of a younger Alexa. I tried many times to converse about various topics but she always managed to relate the topic back to her son. Blankness slowly spreads across her eyes; I must watch her carefully and consider her every behavior.

I left Fleur with a servant in the library and sat alone on the balcony in wait of Isabelle. Time passed and when she still hadn't arrived I asked Kurya if he was aware of her absence. He told me he had met her long ago in the afternoon and used my advice to turn her away for the time being. That irritated me, but I controlled my tongue and hid my anger. Audrey's lessons have been cancelled for the time being. The family will soon grow familiar to this sudden environment and then I will persuade Audrey to call back Isabelle for her lessons. I can feel sleep coming, so I will end this entry here.

17 September

It has been three days Since Alexander left us. The house is, as expected, still haunted. The days now seem to drag on. I am for most of the hours left to myself as the family is still occupied with grief. Victor's unique library has occupied me; in fact I have by now read a bit of his every text to pass the time. A young footman by the name of Maxim joins me during his free time and bombards me with questions regarding my work. Since this afternoon I have begun teaching him the simple ethics and values of psychology, if interested I suppose I could lead him further into this study. His fascination with thought is admirable, but amusing. I "inspire" him he says. Quite honestly, I am too tired of these mediocre compliments for my work; what good, for example, have I brought to this family?

Victor seems to have recovered slightly. He can walk but hardly, his ankle is swollen and an old, rather grumpy, 'Doctor Bora' has placed him on temporary bed rest. Victors mood I'm afraid is only worsening the condition. I hope for his recovery. He still has not forgotten about his guest, in fact he invites me every day to drink with him at his study. We then in the evenings walk through the gardens humming and sharing our memories, and we laugh. What a beautiful sound it is to hear him laugh. Though considering the doctor's advice, I don't appreciate Victor's scheme to make me a part of his little escapes and adventures away from the house, Doctor Bora always seems to blame me with his disapproving gaze, and Victor simply looks away hiding his smile! What a clever, stubborn fool, Victor.

Alexander has not written, but still Victor every morning sends a servant to check the mail, and then he sends another to check again not much later. I have tried to comfort him on this matter and implored him to calm himself, but he simply nods and smiles and continues this sad behavior the very next day. Fleur on the other hand does seem to be getting along quite well, though her behavior at times is questionable and odd. She spends many hours in Alexander's room knitting and reading. An occasional hum resonates from within. She eats only when offered, and only speaks (but not profoundly) when spoken to; it is at times heartbreaking to see.

My deepest concern however, lies with Audrey. She has again joined the company of the house, but not completely or all too enthusiastically. This situation is not only affecting her love and care for Alexander, but it is also affecting her ambitions and her future. Because of her mood she has lost the wonder and curiosity she once expressed for artistic beauty. Slowly she is growing frail, pale and fainéant. She smiles but hardly, and no longer do I hear the happy tunes she once sang so joyously. Today, however, she was in a better spirit. In the afternoon as I passed the piano room, I happened to see her sitting at the instrument where her fingers danced quietly above the keys. I approached her and the touch of my hand on her porcelain clothed shoulder seemed to have calmed her and had her relinquish a pretty little tear. I said nothing but joined her at the seat, where I then began to terribly play a strange sounding rhythm. She laughed, and how soothing it was to hear her do so. Then she too touched the keys, but did little to improve upon my atrocity. Our desperate attempt to create comprehendible music reminded us both of Isabelle. Audrey asked me whether or not she should continue her lessons, and I said she should, but now I wonder if my feelings for Isabelle may have influenced my answer. I *am* excited to see Isabelle, of course, but not at the expense of my care for this family. Already I can feel a growing excitement to spend time with Isabelle. Already I acknowledge the advantage of Alexander's absence to get close to Isabelle, and my God I am ashamed! This racing mind of mine is dangerous and vicious and I must learn to ignore the subtle but cruel ideas of it, if not for me, then at least for the sake of this family.

20 September

I had some time with Maxim today. Victor was called into a sudden meeting with his partners, and although it was difficult to watch him struggle about the house and the town in his condition, it was ever more difficult preventing him from attending the meeting and instead resting at home. Nonetheless he left, and for some time too. Fleur had accompanied him and I think it was the best decision, for he hardly needs to be left alone; who knows what he might urge to do without the proper guidance. Needless to say Doctor Bora was in a paralyzing shock to hear Kurya tell him of Victor's decision, and of course he glared at me, as what I can only assume to be his natural response at this point. Audrey consoled the man, who could hardly walk as he tried to comprehend the disobedience we displayed by letting his patient roam free with a wounded limb; it was actually rather sweet to think of the doctors care for Victor, one that transcends professionalism.

Having the house under my unofficial command was a kind gesture by the servants. They willingly attended to my needs, and displayed the sort of behavior and care only one under the house of Victor would provide. Knowing me to be a dear friend of the family, the servants were unconditionally attentive and sweet. Seeing this sort of care only demands my admiration for the family, for not every employer is as loved and honored by their servants, and not every guest is treated like a king in the absence of the homeowner. Yes, it wasn't the salary that motivated this young crowd, it wasn't the superficial hierarchies set forth by economic borders, it was a pure love; a love for the people who have treated them as family.

But the young man, Maxim, he is interesting. He is indifferent to the altruistic formalities and lacks a natural charm for hospitality, but curse me if he isn't the greatest servant for the conditional salary. But regardless he is condescending to his career, often remarking with subtlety the futility of his position, the hopelessness he sees in the gleaming faces of his fellow workers as they "let the family dehumanize them." He is an intelligent young man, striving for more than where he is. But I'm afraid his perspective and attitude is questionable and disheartening, at times, despite how right he may be. He has no heart for what he does, often looking at the family with contempt, with envy...and well, why should he not? Is it not by the likes of them that this system of rank still exists? Yes they gave them homes, let them read and let them eat, but still, do they not condemn them to this life of service? Were I not the lucky friend, would I not be just another servant, as they look down upon us with a condescending smile? Still, I felt a slight discomfort with my supporting his negligence for his duties, duties he was very much paid for. He sat with me today as I studied in the library. Perhaps I should not have allowed him, for he ignored his duties and chores to be with me, and to speak to me on the topics of my career. But I realized then, as I do now that he cannot always live in this disappointing life, despite how fruitful it may be for the family, and so, I humored his curiosity.

He is amusingly pretentious, and listening to him speak so impertinently about his endeavors to understand the lesser man is shocking. Yet he somehow convinces me of his claims and beliefs by some form of empirical finding, and well, being the researcher that I am, I certainly cannot argue with the quantitative method; was the body not cut to see its heart? He had tried proposing theories that both supported and contradicted my own studies, and although it was insulting to be contradicted by a man of his stature, it was still impressive to hear a simple footman speak intelligently. I lent him one of my books on the matter of the mind, and the concept of a *psyche*; an unconscious that has become quite the topic of question in the field. He was thankful, and bashful, in his own way. Kurya eventually found us both and demanded Maxim to return to his duties, to which the boy gave me a bemused look, as one would give a child, one that was, to say in the least, insulting to his superior in command. And then he left, leaving me as I am now, both impressed and disappointed by the young man.

As maxim left to attend to his duties, he whispered of some artwork I should invest my time in. A certain collection has found itself in the realms of the Zaria residence, and so, being the curious one I am, I will look into finding this art starting to-morrow. Rembrandts sketches are, after all, among my favorites of his creations.

23 September

At breakfast today I was hesitant to ask Victor of Rembrandts whereabouts, for surely such delicate pieces would be under the strict considerations of safety and caution. Though I did manage to express my enthusiasm for them through a very subtle blurt, or two, and Victor grinned and chuckled, (a rarity for these days) and asked me if I was willing to see his temporary collection. And well, could I really deny a friends request?

He led me through the library and towards a door I hadn't had the urge to exploit until now. Upon our reaching of it, Victor looked around and whispered his desire to keep the contents a secret from the help. I understood and agreed and followed him through. Immediately I was hit with the worldly colors, and a sudden romanticism mystified the air as I travelled through it with wilded eyes. The greats, the mediocre and even the failures of their times rested upon the walls of this congested room, and although modest was the collection, it perfectly captured the geography of the artistic world, from the east to the west and the north to the south; from a single vase from a tomb in Ur, to an originally carved blueprint of a Roman aqueduct, and from that to the skillful articulations of Al-Haytham, and ultimately, to a subjective hierarchy of the baroquen greats on the furthest wall of the room; Victor had it all.

"Careful, Alim, I need you sane." Victor mocked as I swept from one side to another, trying my greatest to remain an 'interested' man. I then listened to a rather knowledgeable lecture from my friend, who swept with me and explained all the details that had escaped my comprehension. He spoke passionately and intelligently; two traits I don't often see positively correlated. And everything he had said was satisfying and it only impressed me to learn more. But eventually into our little venture I had come to the realization that the purpose of my coming here was left unanswered, and so Victor led me to a drawer and exposed a neatly lined row of sketches. "Behold: Rembrandt! However, these are only replicas, my friend. But although replicas, they still hold the value in my eyes, for none of the beauty has been taken away from them. In fact, and you may laugh, but these specific replicas are what the Dutch intended to display for the public. But I have a friend at their original home, and well, he stole these for me. Now, now, don't give me that look! They never actually found out, and are in fact ignorantly displaying the original sketches!" Victor bellowed.

"You're a hero, my friend, bringing the originals to the people. Though I hope you didn't acquire everything here in the same manner, I'd hate to think you traversed the ruins of Mesopotamia to grab that pot."

"Oh no, no, that I…found." He said staring at it inquisitively. "So, I will leave you to it. Stare to your heart's content, and if you feel the need to weep I have a lovely little chair in that corner. I apologize for leaving you today, Alim, but I am, unfortunately, desired at my business." And with that we gave our goodbyes and he left me to my wonders. I spent some more time surveying the unseen pieces, and read in greater details of the work I had only but awed at previously, and all this through the handwritten 'biographies' of each piece written by none only than Victor; one must admire the scholar that hides within the leisurely skin of the man.

It was time I approached Rembrandt and confronted the hesitancy that denied me its presence, for it is quite natural to be disturbed in face of the frighteningly human characteristics presented to us; it is art to feel an empathetic response through a sketch of an eye, for aren't artists the translators of emotion? And if so, Rembrandt is the poet of the sorrow; I feel at one with his drawn figures, for they express my very thought and sentiment, and today's opportunity proved nothing less of it.

I had chosen the most projective of the sketches lined, and carefully carried them with their wooden protectors over to the weeping chair mentioned earlier. It is funny, to me the most 'projective' of the pieces were those of weary and aged men, men I can only imagine had seen their light of day, and that many years ago. It is curious to me as to why it was these specific pieces that attracted me, for I was stunned by their complexity. I had perhaps seen parts of myself drawn into them, but parts I am afraid to identify. How clever of Rembrandt to have one introspect through escapism, for I was drawn unto my heart. I turned from one sketch to another, from man to man, from age to age, and that then consecutively, constructing a time lapse of sorts, constructing a single man by the ordering of each mans tragedy, to an ultimate profile of one whose visage was the representation of…guilt? Regret? Is this what Rembrandt designed? Or were these sketches but desperate attempts for his self-expression? But why was *I* afraid? These sketches were not me! I am manipulating a single empathetic response into something personal, and adopting it. How perfect of me to spoil even the reveling of art by self-questioning. Agata's death was a natural one, and my constant burdening myself of it is hurtful. Yes, truly it was the work of a genius to have me possessed by the dimples and the scars, nothing but admiration. Nothing but admiration. How could I have known? I could have known, dared I asked.

To Master Zaria,

Is that what they call you now? Don't let the power get to your head, now. But in all honesty, Victor, I am so proud of you. You have done nearly all that you endeavored, and I am sure that your parents would be proud as well; you have done good by them, my friend, may they rest well. It has been so long since we have seen each other, and my God, how things have changed. I have nearly completed my studies as well, and have been working with some questionable names in the field, and let me tell you that I have never been more curious for the mind as I am now. The studies I undertake, the people I meet, the things I am forced to do, it is terrifying, yet oddly satisfying at the end of the day. Though I doubt I will survive the consequences of this career, so remember me as I was!

Agata is fine, thank you for asking. I am not sure what exactly she is studying now, for she hardly bothers discussing it with me at this point, since I insult its very standing, and better for it! You know I don't care for the topics of her studies. She can be so stubborn at times, supporting her mediocre scholars and fighting me over their contributions to the intellectual world. You know, it annoys me at times to have to face her in this regard, and to always see her so enthusiastic for nonsense. At times, I feel distant from her, unsentimental even, though only sometimes. Needless to say, it is difficult for me to speak with her. Is this wrong? But I should not be telling you this; it is the quarrels of marriage. In other news, tell me about this 'Fleur', I am eager to know more.

-Alim

25 September

I don't think I should stay here for much longer. The atmosphere of this place is haunting and depressing and I am emotionally burdened. Today especially has left me vulnerable to the cruel manipulations of the heart, but, Isabelle condemns me here! Alexander is still gone and silent, so what good would my staying here do? I spend my days planning trips to the city, of course I never do act upon these plans, but instead spend hours reading Alighieri or Ansari in that damned library. I sit in that chair in the corner and stare out of that window and think about her. Maxim continues to show interest in Psychology and bugs me for answers. In fact, he reminds me that I have not once this entire trip written to my hospital or even thought of my patients back home. That alone should be an answer to my pending question of whether or not I should abandon this study. Not only have I been negligent to inquire after them, but I have lost much of the wonder the deviant had always captured me with. What I fear, actually, is that I feel more of an understanding for them than I ever have before. What scares me is that it's not knowledge or study that permits my newfound understanding, but rather, an odd, peculiar *empathy*.

My breakdown earlier this evening leaves me pondering. Never have I felt so pathetic! So desperate! Agata's death is driving me mad. I am losing control of all sense. The only thought that consumes me is of Isabelle, but then I think of Agata and the treatment she bore from me and I can't help but question the desire I have for the girl. This feeling cannot be the simple need to compensate for my mistake! It has to be love! Otherwise I wouldn't have ridiculed Alexander. My head is spinning and I am full of doubt and confusion, but I know one thing clearly, whatever it is that I feel, I must have Isabelle. Today's experience has confirmed this.

I was in my room reading when a servant came to my door. It was evening and Victor had sent the boy to tell me that he wanted me. I assumed this call was for our daily walk, the weather was fine and I had no reason to excuse, and so I accepted the invite and dismissed him. Not much later, after I dressed to face my friend properly, I left. The halls were, as noted, rather desolate, and a certain discomfort bore within me, a fear from the invisible I felt watch me stride. The scent of musk incense burned from the rooms and mixed with the aroma of wet rose roaming through the open shutters, and it bore in me a sudden excitement for the gardens, so I hurried up to Victors room. I reached the top of the steps and stood a mere ten or so feet from the door, which was slightly ajar and from within shone a dim light. I heard Victor's voice whisper, and Kurya's, and I heard my name and Alexander's too. Curiosity and fear drove me, so I crept to the door and concentrated on the voices within. Through the little opening the door established, I noticed Kurya sitting at Victor's desk, pen in hand and paper in front. I could also see Victor's legs on the bed, and as noted, I could hear his voice. I then realized that Kurya was writing a letter for his master. Victor could hardly manage the tremble in his voice, but he spoke nonetheless and his loyal man I assume wrote every word. This is what I managed to hear, this simple thing that insults me:

"*...Alexander, last time we spoke, which feels to me long ago, we spoke of love. I saw it in your eyes, there is a passion glistening. You have always had a gleam in your eyes, but this time it was illuminating, obvious to me. So now I will speak to you of something I think you should hear, not of the war and not of the sentiment burdening you, but rather of love and faith, for that is what awaits you. Read these words carefully: Do not fall in love with this world. Do not let the arts we celebrate or the science we study consume you; for they are only temporary. Yes you may embrace them, study them and enjoy them by all means, but do not let this world define you. Love is found upon the soul, not on the body. What good would exploiting the worldly arts do for you? You could replicate, no, interpret, or perhaps even evolve the sound of Chopin or Debussy, but why would your beloved care, if she is in wait for the majestic, divine love of what's to come? Of Heaven! A place where everyone is equal, a place where you and your neighbor are alike in moral and respect, tell me then, Alexa, how does your irrelevant knowledge and skill compare to that of the indiscriminate love born in your beloved by God? If for example, were men and women and children to bow to your feet tomorrow at the sound of your strings, why would your beloved care if she* *waits for and dreams of divine love, a love of the eternal heart, not of the temporal mind?..."* A love of the eternal heart, not of the temporal mind; these words will never leave my mind, for they have a certain quality about them that touches me. Yet they challenge my very moral, so why then am I condemned to their ringing memory?!

I do not remember the remainder of the letter, for I was dissociate, lost within a world of chaos as I struggled to find the answers to my mistake, the reason for my ruin, the evil that conjured the disgust I felt for the family. He then finished his speech and a sudden silence followed that brought me my attention. I looked in and noticed Kurya preparing the envelope. Victor still lay on his bed, and I heard him ask *Fleur* what she thought of the letter. I hadn't even noticed she was there until Victor said her name and asked her opinion. I peeked in further and saw her sitting on the bed by his side. She said it was fine, and expressed not much more than that. Victor then took her hand in his and smiled at her. She raised his hand to her lips and held it there for some time; she then brushed his hair to the side with her fingers and straightened his folded collar. I heard him weep, and apologize, and then he turned away from her. She kissed his hand again and smiled sympathetically. I could have walked in then, should I have? I could not either way; Victor's letter, and Fleurs care for her husband left me overwhelmed and hesitant to exploit my presence. The last thing I needed then was to face them; I can only imagine what they must think of me! A man without love, consumed with nothing but…nothingness?

I left the door untouched and quietly made my way back to the steps. From there I staggered back to my room as I fought the racing thoughts spinning through my mind. I figured another servant would soon come again, and this time to express Victor's desire to walk, but it was odd, because I *anticipated* it. I fell into the chair out looking the window in my room and waited patiently, feeling the pulsing blood in my veins slowly take hold of me. Sure enough a servant did come and I accepted the invite and dismissed him, but remained in my seat. The sun was setting and the sky was darkening, but I sat still in my chair waiting again for the servant to come. One last time, the same footman reminded me to meet Victor; I dismissed him but did not dare to move. I in fact straightened and looked out inquisitively into the yard where Victor and I walk through, and I waited some more. It was dusk and little sunlight shone, but I knew Victor and his stubbornness, so I searched the yard. Moments later, exiting from the door I saw him. From my window I could just make out his features, and his large figure and terrible limp was unmistakable. With a sick satisfaction I watched him stumble and limp across the yard and disappear into the gardens; he was alone.

I fell into my chair and fidgeted as I tried to understand why I did what I just did. It was completely dark now and the gardens could hardly be seen. I pulled my curtains to a close and stood in the middle of my room with no absolute purpose. My lungs heaved my breaths and my palms began to sweat, a heavy feeling climbed my throat and my head began to spin and pulse with pain…I began to cry. Weakness spread over me and I fell to my knees. A case lay on my bed, so I crawled to it, sobbing, and began searching for some relaxants. I dug through the papers and the folders looking for anything to soothe the disease, and it was then, as I scavenged the leather, that a picture of Agata fell onto the back of my hand. I fell into a nauseating paralysis; the feeling in my throat breathed out, and I bawled, with not a care for any ears listening in to my tragedy. I held the picture in my trembling hands in front of me but could not face it directly. It was guilt, it could not have been anything else…how could I have known! Her eyes looked into me, blatant sadness shone in them, yet, she was smiling.

Despite the years of unhappiness and sorrow she experienced, she was smiling in the picture she took for me. And her lips, her expression, as I was in her thoughts; her still relentless façade of joy, for me. Did she see the good in me? Did she seek it through this plea? But she died without my seeing it…until now, and how beautiful it is, my dear loves smile. It took me some time to breathe again, and stop the tickling of the tears, but when I did, I kissed the picture and placed it deep into the case. I then climbed up onto my bed; my cheeks felt moist and my chest warm, and powerful sleep whelmed me. Before I fell completely into unconsciousness, Isabelle came to my mind, and I heard her laugh and I knew then that I needed her.

It is morning, the sun has just risen and only now can I hear the servants waking above me. I am seeing Isabelle today, finally. I will wait and see how much more I can control, I must endure for her.

27 September

Everything seems to me much clearer now, more than ever. I have acknowledged my love for Isabelle rather than avoiding my feelings as I had been doing with such endeavor. Because of this a sort of sanity has whelmed me. Also, because of the family's growing weakness, I have now an odd sort of empowerment over them. They trust me, and I have been, despite however wrong it is, been taking advantage of them. I see them when I need to, this being when I need their car or some other of their luxuries, otherwise I avoid them. Victor is still constrained to bed, and as I had expected, his mental state has only frustrated if not forsaken his chance for absolute recovery. It is so ironic to see that I alone keep their spirits alive; the very sight of me swells in their cheeks a glimmering Nur. This, in fact, is one reason for why I avoid them, the guilt I feel and the shame that embowers me is one I cannot bare in their face. Another reason for my negligence is being that I have, almost cruelly, lost all familial affection for them; they are now but just familiar faces. But Victor's good faith in me is ever so proven through his ignorance of the fact that I have been rejecting him and our walks to spend more time with Isabelle. I am sure he does feel a sort of abandonment when I decline or shamefully ignore his invitations to drink or to the gardens, but because of his love for me, he doesn't question. Still, out of the respect of the friendship he still believes I care for, just yesterday I had brought him a cane from the city. He uses it now to stroll around his home, mostly roaming the halls of his children, and trying to motivate his daughter. Audrey is still overwhelmed. Even though she has begun again her lessons, Isabelle tells me that Audrey's effort is diminishing and the poor girl grows tired of it all; I am afraid of when she will. Fleur is hopeless, what more can I say. She is still quiet and somewhat dissociate. Alexander has not replied to his father's letter, nor has he written in general. It is becoming clear now that the boy is probably dead. Of course this possibility is never spoken of, but it is so well acknowledged through the cries of the mother or the dead prayers of the sister. If he is not dead, then surely he has run off and away from battle, I am afraid to say that his very personality was of the sort.

I have been discreet in my time spending with Isabelle. The last thing I want is for this tormented family to know I have abandoned them for their daughter's tutor. I have been accompanying her to the city after her lessons with Audrey, and sometimes we take the path through the gardens, laughing and coming closer to one another every day. I feel ashamed in the fact that Isabelle too feels guilt in spending good time with me while the grievous grieve, for it is I who initiates our time spending. But I honestly cannot help the urge, the desire, to be with her. I am hesitant to confess my feelings just yet; I am not sure exactly how she feels of me. I was never much of a romantic and a woman's heart has always been a most convoluted thing to me. I will wait.

2 October

Isabelle and I have finally established a bond for intimate conversation. I spoke to her of Agata today. I hardly wanted to, but the poor girl had had enough of formalities, and curiosity and wonder had possessed her. Not only am I relieved to have liberated my heart from sentimental tether, but her sudden fascination with my private life is only but inspiring to me. I still yearn to hear from her lips the confessions of passion, as she does from me. But I, as I am sure she is of me, am confident about her feelings. For today, and the most beautiful moment of it, spoke to me of the love her heart is bound to secrecy for.

I was waiting, as I regularly do now, for Isabelle and Audrey to end their musical session. Audrey was of course still discontent and fairly scorn with sadness, yet she trudged through the lesson for the sake of politeness and the kindness her nature has always shown, and is, without a doubt, composed of. Isabelle dared not to end the session, *her* nature is of feminine inclination for amelioration, and therefore she believed the musical poems of her strings were but all that Audrey's heart needed. Who was I to interfere with a woman's ideology! So I sat nearby and watched them practice for the hour, studying Audrey's eyes for even a spark of enthusiasm to appear; could she not have at least appreciated the effort Isabelle had given? Yes she was burdened, I know, but I'm sure she hurt Isabelle with her behavior.

After the lesson had concluded, Audrey thanked her tutor and inadvertently ignored me as she left the room, obviously relieved. Isabelle was dubious and questioned her persistence to me, I consoled her. I then asked her the anxious request for a stroll through the gardens, for the weather was warm and bright and passionate, and so was I. She agreed, unhesitant and joyous, and so we left the house and wandered through the grass leading into the array of the blinding colors, which are usually quite dull and dead at this time of the year. As we walked away from the house and towards the garden, I was eager to avoid the gaze of the house. But upon my urge to look behind, I thought I noticed for a second the face of Victor looking down upon me from his window view. I was wrong, and continued onto the floral paths with Isabelle by my side.

Her spontaneous and heartwarming laughs were inspiring, and the trembling, hesitant and excited voice that spoke her words was invoking and titillating. I wish I could forever more relive or feel again the moments that followed. The first little path of the gardens was of light brown marble, and it led to another and another, like streams flowing through green fields commonly do. The colors of this atmosphere, the green, the reds, yellows and the occasional hues of blue were almost as if Isabelle and I were the first ever to witness them, and our child-like eyes wandered through them all. The path we chose seamlessly passed through over-reaching arches of dark colored orchids. Each arm of green formed over and touched above our heads as we walked under them, numb with thrill. She spoke first.

"Did you love Agata?" she hid her eyes from mine, and instead looked towards and touched her hand through every passing leaf. Love to me, as I have noted, has always been a sort of mystery. The 'love' I feel for her now, that love is one rooted in jealousy and betrayal, so what could I tell her? But I humored the girl, and spoke to her after some consideration.

"I believe, Isabelle, that at some time, a part of me did. To exaggerate my devotion would be unjust, and if I were to do so, I would be ashamed. The word for Love is a mysterious one too, so I cannot blindly speak the word, for I know nothing of its nature. There is love that hues the cheeks and flusters the voice, there is love that drums the heart. There is love that has one sacrifice, for good and for bad. Then there's love worth dying for, sometimes worth killing for. Some love is rooted in pure happiness, and sometimes rooted in jealousy, other times in stupidity! And then, Isabelle, there is also the love of love, an infatuation with just the philosophy of it! Of course, that however is an entirely different science of sentiment." I smiled, but she hadn't turned to me, and as she continued her behavior with the leaves I spoke again. "But please understand me; I am sure that whatever love you speak of, Agata had felt that for me. And that, dear Isabelle is what I am most ashamed of. So I suppose if there is one thing you should know about me, is that I am completely oblivious to the entire idea of emotion. But, you have asked me and I have answered, so, what is *love* to you?" To this she did turn, a ridiculing smile formed on her lips, and she spoke.

"Isn't that a bit ironic for *you* of all people to say? Anyways, love itself is what I am asking about. Its roots are known only to its victim and God. The choice to act upon one's love is also between that of the possessed and God. But love is a simple thing, despite its roots. To me, love is breathlessness and helplessness; obsession, yes? A feeling that wakes you in the morning, and also dabs you to sleep at night. A feeling that can hardly be understood by science and only accepted by spirit. So I don't think you are oblivious to the idea of love, but rather you're afraid of it. The Orientals, for example, have many words for love! And if you were honestly curious of its philosophy, you would certainly know that." Afraid? I am only afraid of what it brings. I admit at this point I was beginning to feel uncomfortable continuing this conversation with Isabelle. I felt naïve, or somewhat immature on the matter of which she spoke; theology has always been beyond my comprehension.

"Perhaps I am just entirely not curious at all." I remarked knowing her flirtatious intricacy. She gave me a titillated look.

"Well that's too unfortunate. I really thought you were, for you certainly give the impression of a man desperate to know."

As we entered a short, dark tunnel of leaf, Isabelle stepped near me and I felt her hand touch mine. As the sunlight showed her face I saw a rosy blemish in her cheeks. She then, smiling and overwhelmed, turned and walked onto the grass and disappeared behind a wall of hedge stretching parallel to the path of which I strode; I was captivated so I stood still, as did her figure. Her fair skin shone through the dark green between us, and the red strands of her hair gleamed through too, like sunlight through water. A Tsarina she was, hiding herself within the walls of Kremlin, though seeing me through and through, gazing. With a drumming heart I peered deep into the leaves, dazed and fluttered. "Why are you hiding?" I asked, with immature curiosity.

I then heard her sweet sound laugh, and she answered. '*Unlike the beauties of your world, with the veil I am seen, but without it I am hidden.*' It made me wonder, but still engrossed by her scene and now with a peculiar modesty I watched her figure stroll across the colored shade of dark green as she retreated from around the hedge and walked to me, smiling. "Jami, *Lawa'ih.*"

That moment, I am sure it will be one of most importance to me. It was a delicate thing, and inspiring, and has certainly given me a sudden form of motivation…for life!

Isabelle and I departed at the town, after which I *walked* back to the Zaria's residence. The air was of great comfort to me and I didn't want to miss a breeze of it. It was evening when I reached them, and the falling sun and the darkening sky were of perfect setting for the atmosphere that breathes this place alive. Only Fleur sat at the dining table when I had arrived. I sat there too and said trivial things to lighten her mood. She said very little in return and only bothered to smile for my sake. I am afraid, that with every passing day this family loses strength and is soon to lose all hope as well.

Alexander is to return; a letter arrived this morning. Kurya implored us to gather into the dining room for his instinct believed the letter to be from Alexander. I was there waiting with a cup of chai as Victor, with the help of fleur, exhaustedly joined us. The man handed my friend the neatly tightened letter and an excitement bore in us all. At first my friend casually ripped open the envelope believing it to be just another newsletter the office sends to the families of the soldiers. However, as he read it I noticed his cheeks drain of all color. This sudden pallor caught the curiosity of both Audrey and Fleur for they at once and together interrogated him in their own respects. He simply put the letter down and looked up to us. He was calm, but clearly shocked as he told us that Alexander is to be coming home. Fleur dropped her cup and reached for the letter. As she read it Audrey too ran up behind her and gazed upon the letter over her mother's shoulder.

I remained at my seat and had lost my appetite. Of course I was happy that the boy is alive and well, but I couldn't avoid the heavy feeling starting in my stomach. I was lost in thought; fear, perhaps relief? I am not sure. But Fleur's terrible shriek upon finishing the letter grasped me back into reality. She dropped the letter and was caught by Audrey as the two women stumbled onto the floor. The boy has been blinded in both eyes and has been sent back home for an obvious incompetency. I watched this scene sitting in my chair with helpless sympathy. Victor hardly moved and hid his face in his hands; beside him on the floor laid Fleur crying painfully, and comforting her was the young daughter.

The rest of the day was rather active. The word of Alexander's return quickly spread through the home and the servants became alive and dutifully enacted upon their responsibilities. Kurya with his everlasting devotion and love for Victor, relentlessly insisted his employer to rest rather than letting him stroll around the home, buried in thought; so much so that Victor at one point even snapped at the loyal man to leave him alone! Kurya simply shook his head, gave *me* an irritated look and left our company in silence. After gathering the strength, Fleur set off with Audrey to the post office in town; I am sure she had some sort of letter for Alexander, or perhaps for the writer of the tale depicting the boy's tragic truth, which so spontaneously arrived this morning, leaving us all desperate for answers. Tomorrow begins the hectic preparation and the anxious trepidation for Alexander's long-awaited return. I will sleep now so that I can rise early enough to contribute my labor. Goodnight.

11 October

Alexander is to arrive tomorrow. We have been preparing for his return. His room has been completely rearranged to support his injury. Few words have been said during the accommodations, for Victor always seems somewhat distracted. He can hardly hold a proper conversation, and I doubt he even cares to. He occasionally mumbles his thoughts as he works on Alexander's new room. I have learned to agree and submit to whatever he says; it is pointless challenging his mediocre demands, for he could care less about whatever is said to him. Fleur seems much more able than her husband. She has conquered her fear for Alexander and is now just excited for her son's return. She paces around the house decorating for Alexander's convenience, and there's always a lovely smile to be found on her lips. Audrey has been under her mother's dictatorial command. She runs from one end to the other fulfilling Fleur's wishes. Surely a girl like Audrey is destined for good fortune. When I find spare time from managing the servants I retire to my room; to slowly overcome my odds with the boy, and slowly begin to long for his return. I will try to sleep, but I fear the dreams that await me will keep me awake; the dreams of facing Alexander with a smile.

12 October

It was a very quiet day, but one with many soft moments worth noting. I had hadn't slept through the night, so my day begun with the beauty of the rising sun enveloping the lands with light. I lay there helpless and afraid as the powerful candescence covered me. I was sure the others had felt it, for I doubt there was any one asleep to have missed it. I dressed formally, smoked an oscuro at the sofa overlooking the landscape, and when I felt brave, I wearily left my silent room to join the company waiting for Alexander below. I reached the first floor to find servants swiftly moving about for last minute preparations. I asked for Fleur and was told she had been preparing in Alexander's room all morning and refused to come down until everything was in perfect order. Audrey had not even left her room as of then, and so I joined Kurya in the dining room. Kurya seemed worried and did not acknowledge me as I said good morning and asked for Victor's whereabouts.

He simply looked out onto the front yard and shook his head; he then did eventually notice me and complained of Victor's stubbornness. I joined his peering and noticed Victor standing outside near the front entrance; he was still in his robes and stood unmoved staring out onto the welcoming path. I left to join him. When I reached him he still stood there terribly worn out and looking rather unkempt; his hair was wild and his eyes were red and tired. I called his name, to which he turned and all too enthusiastically invited me to join him in the fair weather. His behavior seemed much too scripted, which was appropriate, for he was considerably burdened with thought and nerve. I humored his dialogue until finally imploring him to join the rest of us inside the home and dress appropriately for the occasion. "Of course, of course!" he said motioning me inside and begging me to go eat breakfast. I obeyed him and left him standing there for another few minutes, until he too finally trudged back inside.

I had no appetite, and as of then the floor was much too hectic, and so I strolled about the home constantly glancing at my watch, for I too began to feel a trembling anxiety. Audrey eventually passed me in the hall, to which she smiled gracefully and happily, as is her behavior upon seeing me; I lighten her cheeks and give life to the sweet visage that speaks her soul. Today however, I did notice that she was terribly stressed and contemplative. I can only imagine how confused and overwhelmed the girl must feel to finding such situations corrupt her life. The weakness in her eyes and the paleness of her color had me beg her to eat something before Alexander arrived. She respected my order and we departed.

I then remembered that I had in fact bought a gift for Alexander just a few days earlier after I learned of his return. I had a bought him a ring. This ring is unique, for it has no design and its green color is a simple thing. But the material of its making is one of wonder. It shines translucently, and expresses beautifully the craftsmanship of its creator; the Chinese. The value of it is not found on its skin, but rather in its impressive truth; a quality I found fitting for a man like Alexander. And so I hurried to my room to collect it. I had just finished folding it when I heard many voices speak loudly below me. I walked to my window and looked out onto the yards and noticed a small, depressingly black car drive along the path towards the house; it was then my heart began to race, for I suddenly realized the realness of this moment. From where I stood I could little but see the front entrance of the home, and witnessed the three members of the family, and Kurya too, standing together and brilliantly formed, but silent and still. I wanted to join them, should I have? It didn't feel right for me to, not just then. And so I watched the car reach us and come to a stop, and from within the backseat stumbled out an old man in a gray suit and tie, with a grey hat, grey scarf and black shoes. He gave a short bow to Victor and turned back to the car. I was so anxious, and so curious that I could hardly stand still as I watched the scene through my window, isolate above them all.

The man then spoke to someone within the car, and slowly, aiding him with every move brought out a young man bandaged from ear to ear; I looked away, a pulse was pulling on my throat and my breathing began to stutter. When I looked again Fleur was holding the boy in her arms and did so for many silent seconds. The old man, to no one's acknowledgement but mine, bowed again, turned and soon drove away in the same black car after handing over the responsibility of Alexander to the two women who grasped him delicately. What is interesting and something I must take note of is that the most moving thing of this scene was the silent sound of it: it was of absolute solace. Neither parent spoke to the son, nor did the sister. But rather the family very solemnly embraced their beloved and helped him into his home. No longer were they to be seen from where I stood, so no longer could I hide myself away up here, away from the mysterious shame that bowered my body and mind.

In a daze I wrapped the little gift; each knot blinding me with an image of the boy's bandaged face. When I felt good and ready and brave I left the room and wandered through the halls towards the floor in which they all stayed, most certainly in wait for me. I was in a state of dread and worry but only until I walked into their room and saw the many smiles of relief and joy, and then did I feel certain warmth overcome me. It grew silent when I said hello, for Alexander's dimples vanished and he straightened his posture at the sound of me, to which Audrey laughed alone. His reaction wasn't of much compliment, but I can hardly blame him; I believe my presence to him is nothing but unsentimental. I was embarrassed, of course, but couldn't stop smiling! I was happy to see him! I hugged the boy and felt him succumb in my arms.

At dinner, Alexander's food was cut to pieces so he could eat comfortably, though he didn't really eat much at all, mostly due to his family's desperate state of curiosity and wonder, but also, I wonder, because of a certain embarrassment. Question after question was thrown at him and he fought them off like a proper soldier. Rather than the war it was of his off duty adventures that we spoke of. He had seen much of the world despite the shortness of his action. Fleur watched her son with precious observation, eyeing carefully his every move and wincing at an almost little accident of a dropped glass. Victor, as he listened attentively to the stories, ate in what I believe was an attempt to compensate for his lost appetite during the last few weeks; I am officially convinced that he considers his belly to be of artistic expression. The frail, young lady seated beside her brother laughed at nearly everything, I suppose she needed an excuse to express her happiness, and Kurya's mediocre sense of humor was of a perfect opportunity! They really were interesting, the stories Alexa spoke of.

He had seen all sorts of people, of music and art, and his vivid memory of them gave us all the pleasure of practically experiencing them too. Victor then asked him of a possible love, and the son's cheeks flushed as he shook his head with a sheepish smile, a reaction which caused some laughs from the company but none from me. I watched him think and smile and breathe, and realized that the thought of Isabelle had kept him alive and brought him home. It was a sweet thing really, but rather disarming, saddening. I did notice something I hope the others did as well, there seems to be a little lesion on Alexa's head under the bandages. I have seen the sort before on my wounded patients. And as they habitually did, Alexa too occasionally blinked anxiously and a little tremble appeared on his lips. It didn't seem to disrupt his emotion however, nor did it distract his happy family. I will watch him and his behavior even though I am sure it is of nothing too harmful.

I am in my room now as I write this entry. It is late and I am tired too, although sleep is of little desire. Everyone has supposedly gone to bed, but I am sure there is another in this house awake as I, writing in their own diaries the 'peculiaritics' of their day. Goodnight.

13 October

Alexander was asleep for most of the day. And rightfully so! I would be worried otherwise. When he did wake he met most of us in the library. It must be strange for him to experience the sudden change of atmosphere. He is very aware of things. He sits almost as if in his own fantasy, but listens to every sound. He spoke only when spoken to, but his speech was not dole or uninterested, but rather enthusiastic and welcoming to a further conversation. When I found him to be in solace, I noticed he would lightly massage his head and oddly wince upon his doing so. This behavior caught the attention of Victor, who asked his son the matter but was answered with an obvious reply.

Before Alexa woke, Isabelle visited us. She was much too eager to see the boy and even suggested waiting all evening to do so. I encouraged her to come again tomorrow at an appropriate time, for Alexander's first day should be with his family. And I also told her it was too soon for Alexander to see someone of little relation. She thought about this but ultimately did take my advice. Audrey even seemed to agree with my proposal. But only I know the truth of this procrastination. Seeing Isabelle be so ignorant of me at her arrival, during her stupor to see the boy, well, it hurt me.

17 October

Victor has suggested I once again begin sessions with Alexander. I was afraid that he would want me to; I am in a much too delicate state myself to be responsible for another. I almost questioned his proposal but I managed to suppress my concern. Instead I asked him why he believes my therapy would be of any use. He consoled me and spoke of how he believes Alexander would only trust to express himself to me. He says I bring in the boy an invigoration of self-expression. His words were lies, for I know the very truths of my capabilities. I am afraid if I continue I will hurt the boy unknowingly. Yesterday, for example, said nothing but the very fact.

When Isabelle came to visit at the time suggested, I left it to Audrey to welcome her in. I anticipated Isabelle's enthusiasm to meet Alexa and I hardly wanted to see it. Even Alexander upon learning of Isabelle's visit begged to see her at the door himself. His caretakers scoffed at the thought. I decided to wait in my room and let the two reunite without me. But my imagination is one of wonder and kept me from staying hidden away for too long. I purposelessly walked through the halls of the home slowly making my way closer to Alexander's room. I neared and heard the two joyful voices from within the room. Stopping at the door I was completely ignored as the two sat in blissful ignorance of their surroundings. Alexa was fascinating her with far-fetched tales of his experiences, as Isabelle seemed to be just happy to see him. "And to think you're still alive!" I interrupted as Alexander boasted. To this they both nearly jumped. I said hello to Isabelle, who for some odd reason had established a little blush in the cheeks. Alexander too had on a silly smile, and took advantage of his blindness by not having to care to hide it from me. "Well don't let me interrupt your story, Alexa. Please continue."

"I don't think I should, actually. You'll know I'm lying. I told you the less-intriguing truth of it yesterday." He said with a little laugh. To this Isabelle nudged him in disapproving humor. I let them speak some more as I sat with a book in my hand but was completely absorbed in their conversations. They too seemed too aware of me and their words seemed emotionless and scripted. Isabelle eventually decided to leave us for it was late. Audrey and I walked the girl to the front and left her there.

I then went back to Alexander's room for a reason I cannot understand. I sat there as he spoke some more of Isabelle and her consideration to see him. I wanted to hide my own admirations, so I merely agreed with his words but said little to build upon them. His state seemed to change as he spoke more and more. His words grew dark and filled with patronizing humor. I said nothing but watched him as he slowly turned vulgar. He began to mock his blindness with humor towards his feelings for Isabelle. I tried to find words of consolation or comfort, yet I was mute with *confusion.* At that moment I myself was struggling to find a mental calming. My silence only encouraged his self-pity for he spoke with no sense and no consideration of my presence. After a long, silent pause he spoke again, but consciously and sorrowfully for me having to hear him. I consoled him. He eventually grew tired and I sat with him until he fell into a deep lumber. I have just recently left him and come to my own room. I am conscious of my incompetence to care for the boy. I can clearly see the difficulties I'm facing in having to console the boy, yet, I have to continue this practice. I have already betrayed Victor far too much.

20 October

My therapy on the boy seems to be progressing well. I have managed to drift the topic of conversation away from his feelings for Isabelle and onto more relevant subjects. Today he spoke of some literature, specifically that of the 'La Vita Nuova' and its poetic form. The desperations of the man within it, the writer of its passionate tragedy, had captured his heart. He spoke then of some music, some history and a little more of theology; a subject he has since become less critical of, and a lot less inquisitive of as well. For the better I suppose, for his faith has become simple and unconditional. But these topics were of not much use to me for our sessions, so instead I asked him of the war, if there was anything specific he wished to discuss about it. To this he paused within a strange pondering. When he spoke, his voice was focused and direct. His words were mature and I knew then that the following had been rehearsed through his mind many times already. Upon learning this I grew eager, enthusiastic almost, to hear his mind on the matter; a feeling I once bore as a younger man in this profession, a feeling I had forgotten I lost. And this time I was prepared to exercise the session and to contribute appropriately rather than letting him fall into a delirious, self-depreciating state. He spoke.

"There is something I want to tell you, Doctor. The story of how I lost my eyes. You see, I'm not as upset about it as I should be, am I? No. That is because I am alive and the others are dead. There were about five, six men like me who were flanked at first. We fought through a growing fog, fought through a rise of foreign voices surrounding us. It was then I felt the fire pierce my sight. It burned into me, a blackening pain hit me. But I still heard all around me, Doctor. I heard the voices of the men I was with, their screams. They were dragged and beaten and killed in front of my blindness and I was…helpless." Alexander now spoke with a disarming voice. No longer did he tear or flutter through the nose as he had long ago, but rather he breathed through a dead tongue. His next words were truly strange. "I'm trying to say, Doctor that I was kept alive as they suffered the unimaginable. So it makes me wonder…am I not capable of their pain? Does God think me so weak to simply burn my eyes and cast me aside as the rest died fighting with swords in hand? As my captured friends silently endured torture, I sit here and cry to you over a woman, a woman I cannot even remember the face of. Am I that small, Insignificant to God? Why am I not there with them? I want to be, I should be. But I am here, in pain from loving a faceless woman who cares nothing for me."

The direct manner in which he spoke only proved his obsession with the thought of suffering. It made me wonder too of my own circumstances. But then I remembered the countless hours I spent striving to accomplish my present self and a sudden pride touched me. So I thought for a moment until speaking to him calmly. "Alexander. Everyone one has their suffering. Pain is unique to the victim. The pain you feel impressively may not even make me wince, nor my pain to you. What would make us unique if we all shared the same experience and suffered through it together? Nothing. And about God, God knows our capabilities better than us I suppose. God wouldn't give us more than we can endure, and everyone endures different pains, for that is the human condition. The men enduring the torture as you say, well, perhaps they couldn't stand the pain of love. Perhaps God knew you would willingly die for your family, die for the sake of honor, more willingly than them. It would be no challenge to you, as it is for them." I then put a hand on his shoulder and spoke with a little humor to make him smile. "Perhaps, Alexander, God knew you were a hopeless romantic." He laughed a little at first and then some more upon thinking of the honesty in the words. Whether he took my words under consideration I do not know, but it was clear to see that my voice alone assuaged him. "And about Isabelle, my dear boy." This was a topic I was hesitant to approach, but seeing him as so empowered me with responsibility. I tried to find a way to reach him through this and suddenly I was given a thought. "Well, why did Beatrice eat her lover's heart?" His brows furrowed with confusion. I watched him think and reflect the image of a younger Victor.

"She didn't" he finally said. "It was just her lover's dream."

"Exactly" I said back to him. "Don't think too much of

something. It will drive you mad and mislead you." He smiled at my mediocre attempt to answer his questioning of Isabelle. "And Lastly, Alexander." I looked into the exact face of a younger Victor now. As the memories of my youth began to overcome my sentiment, I put a weary hand on his shoulder and I *heard* my voice speak these words: "Don't compare yourself to others, Alexa."

These sessions with Alexander of late have been of a benefit to us both. I have managed to carry conversation away from Isabelle, for the most part anyways, and it seems to finally unveil the purpose of my being here. Contrary to what I had believed, Isabelle still acknowledges the friendly relationship we had built upon Alexander's absence. In fact I think Isabelle may even seem a bit more expressive than she was before. Many times I see her distracted by a thought. She then opens her mouth to speak but ultimately keeps silent with hesitation. If I only I knew the secrets of her contemplation. Perhaps she is waiting for me to speak my mind. I notice she doesn't rush me, for the memory and love of Agata is still present in me. She only occasionally visits Alexander now, and when she does it is only for brief moments of kind formalities. It is for the best that she quickly ends this mysterious infatuation between her and Alexander, it is best for us all, despite how cruel.

24 October

And just as my relationship with Alexander began to develop, I betray my sanity and commit the violence of today! Was there a purpose for such cruelty? What game is my heart playing with my mind? No, it couldn't have been so deliberate. It happened by chance and my sensitivity is simply overcoming my reason. Perhaps writing it here will exploit the secrets of its nature:

I woke in the morning, it was nearing noon yet the sky was darker than its usual hue for the hour. The day followed the common routine. Most of it was spent with Victor in the library. It is interesting, one would think that a life of luxury would satisfy the curiosities of the mind, yet Victor promotes the idea of exploration everyday with his reading of books and foreign scripts. Today he spoke to me on the importance of 'cultural' history. An aspect of history often ignored in the classroom, often overshadowed by a 'political' history. I do agree with him on the matter, we are blind to the colors of our neighbors but think we know well the arts of their hand. It was evening soon and it is usually at this hour I plan the sessions with Alexander, so I left Victor to his research and set myself for the visit to his son. After a quick roam through the halls thinking of the coming session, as is my nature before any session, I finally reached the room of Alexander. But from within I heard Audrey imploring her brother to cooperate in his treatment. She has begun helping Alexander physically accustom to his situation by having him walk and find his feet without his eyes guiding him. I didn't want to interrupt the two, so I waited outside for them to finish.

A servant walked in and I heard Isabelle's name from within. Audrey dismissed the man, said some words to her brother and then followed the footman out the door and down the steps to the first floor. She was ignorant of me as I waited parallel to the door of the room. I was in little mood to see Isabelle today, admittedly, a little fever burned through me and I hardly wanted to exercise my senses. Since the girl was coming today at this hour, I decided to use her as an excuse to postpone the session for another day. I walked to the opening of the room and almost spoke until I saw the sight and froze at the door in silence. Alexander stood feet away from his bed across the room. He supported himself by placing a hand on a cabinet table beside him. His standing figure at the moment reminded me of a younger Victor; proud, confident, arrogant. I suppose the boy was left by his sister in the stance and most likely told to wait for her return. I just watched him. I observed his mumbling and thinking. To see him alone in a world of his imagination was beyond interesting, so I said nothing but watched hesitantly from not so far away. He called out suddenly his sister's name. He mumbled and laughed under his breath while cursing her.

He let go of the table and began to stumble with his feet as he walked into darkness, arms in the lead. His lame manner of it all was captivating and watching him was terrifyingly *satisfying*. It was sad too, in a way, to watch his legs falter as he gradually wandered through the room: Alexander the dancing blind man. I noticed the number of chairs in his way and began to anticipate his crossing them. However wrong it was to be fascinated by the scene, the biggest mistake of mine was letting it run on for far too long. I let him hit the chair with his shin, at first he stumbled some more but ultimately lost his balance and fell to the ground to hit his head against the leg of the bed. He gave out a little grunt as he threw his clenched fingers to the lesion on his head. I was late, yes, but I did step in to help him. As I neared he was still unaware of my presence, for he moaned to himself as he crawled across the floor touching the side of the bed with a hand. He stopped and began to mumble something unintelligently under his breath, which again grew my interest. I let him speak. But he seemed delirious, for his words were meaningless to me and his consciousness was foreign. He flipped onto his back and again grasped his head, trembling.

I was confused and shocked by both what I had seen and what I had done. As I stood immobile in the center of the room I heard voices from the hall echo within. The voices of Audrey and Isabelle came near and prompted me to rush to Alexander's side. "Alexander!" I yelled as the girls walked in. Isabelle shrieked and stood at the door with what I assume was fear. Audrey too screamed her brother's name as she ran to his side and helped me prop him to bed. He was clenching his fists and fighting an invisible war in his mind. Isabelle had called for some others; meanwhile Audrey and I attempted to constraint her fidgeting brother. He hit her head as he suddenly wailed his arm and yelled an insult in her direction. I doubt he was aware of his actions, yet the poor girl victim to his attack stood aside, weeping.

"It's my fault for this, I pushed him to do this, now look!" She said within a frantic cry. Is there no depth to my cruelty?

"No, no, Audrey. Don't blame yourself for this." I said constraining Alexander. "He is a fool and impatient for ignoring us." She was still in panic as the others came in the room and took over the responsibility from me. I watched Isabelle rush past me and grab Alexander's hand in hers. Eventually he calmed and drifted into a sleep. The others were afraid of his sudden composure, but I assured them of its peace. Isabelle, shaken and upset, left us after fulfilling her usefulness, with not a single word to me. She wished to see Audrey but the poor sister had gone up to her room and kept silent from us all. Later in the night, Fleur sat by her sleeping son as Victor and I discussed the workings of the sudden accident: a terrible thing it was.

27 October

Alexander has changed. He is ill-tempered, upset and full of rude wit. I know though, of course, it is humiliation he feels. He feels us staring; watching him carefully like one would watch a child; because so, he doesn't speak much to his family. So I have advised them to let him breathe. He does though, ironically, speak to me, and preferably too. I have recurred to my poor manner of therapy. A looming guilt keeps me from saying much to the boy. Our sessions are one-sided and the material of it is dull. He speaks no more of Isabelle and I hardly even notice in his eyes the love he once sung. Audrey is still motivated to the promise of recuperation, but Alexander is losing his. Although motivated, Audrey seems almost ashamed to speak to Alexander. I am sure she still blames herself for the previous incident. Alexander ignores any mention of it. He humors Audrey's commitment, and now with a brusque attitude towards the girl. Their relationship seems weak and is deteriorating by the day. Audrey too will soon lose interest or care to invigorate the boy. Alexander himself has felt the change in their relationship. He feels distant to her and his parents too. He told me once of how he feels as a burden in the house. Perhaps I could have said more to reason with him, but no, he would've seen through my mediocre reassurance anyways.

The lesion on his temple has enlarged since the incident. I must note that as we speak in the sessions Alexander is constantly touching it. He winces and grunts too but says nothing of it. Some of the others have taken note of it as well, but Alexa answers their curiosities with attitude. I have kept silent on the matter; I wish to watch his behavior and am afraid of any reason to change the natural order of the wound. I will continue to track all I have been writing about. I also hope, considering the atmosphere of late, that the family does not lose themselves.

October 29

Alexander dismissed me, I agreed and that was it; a simple thing. Was I to dispute him with a superficial concern? No, Alexa has acknowledged for some time now the formality to his father that carried our 'sessions', and he has grown bored of indulging it. So I did as he desired, something which came as a relief to me and an indifference to him. Victor is ignorant of the thing, though I doubt he hardly bothers for it at all now. He has taken it upon himself to care for the boy in all respects. He even joins him for every meal in the boys' room, the two alone; this being because of Alexa's and Audrey's quarrel at dinner a couple of nights ago. Audrey, I assume growing absolutely worn out by Alexa's mediocre stamina during her endeavors, lashed out at him that night, after quipped of his nihilistic quotes. Alexa was quiet through the taunting; a careless smile was his answer. This angered Audrey; she spoke like I never would imagine her too. She insulted her brother with all in present, and it took the stern voice of her mother to silence her. Needless to say that the girl has abandoned her trying to help Alexa, nor has she even spoken to her brother since this. Victor was silent but humiliation tinted his cheeks, and I know that he could feel my stare. Anyways, this moment above all can be the example of the change that has overcome the personality of this home.

I stay here because of Isabelle, because I can, and because I want to for her. She doesn't come now as the lessons have been all but forgotten. Instead I meet the girl in the town and we spend the few hours of the noon doing trivial things. It's a nice time for me, and I can tell that she feels the same. I'm tired now and this entry may be my last, for there is nothing really worth writing for now. Still, I will keep it with me and if I live to the age, I will look back and laugh at my "romantic" adventure.

31 October

There was a patient once, what was his name? Henry I believe. Yes, I've been thinking about him. I remember his insanity and how he was considered to be the worst of man. The crimes he had done, happily, euphorically in fact, as if it was his natures drink. He was given to me for care. For a time I labeled his incompetency and kept him in the room in wait for his execution, for there was nothing else to be done. But it was interesting, how he *changed.* He began to act and speak like a child once, and another time spoke to us of his mother, as if she were alive and well waiting back home for him. I never did understand completely the nature of his mental regression, but it intrigued me then just as it does now. For a man so tainted with innocent blood, he soon came to forget the pursuing of his sins. By his fifth year with me, he was lost into a world of his own, a world of his memories, a world of his absolute innocence. Soon he forgot his name too, and his age and his sense of self. He grew infatuated with a nurse, well, at least on the days he could remember her. He wrote horrible poetry and at night he would cry alone in his cell, scared, asking for answers to his captivity.

But he was truly happy in this state, the sort of happiness I witnessed myself on his face the day of his condemnation, the day he still was considered "sane", as ironic as that may sound. He was a different person by the time he died, and because of this I was given overwhelming regard and praise for my work, something I had accepted out of a confusing pride. I watched him till the day he was executed, and by then he was dissociate, untouched by the sound of reality. Was he still guilty? He adopted, upon his imprisonment, a new world, a new sense of life and it practically changed him. I don't think he should be considered so. What a beautiful feeling it must be to become anew, to obliviously forget the sins of your hands. I've been thinking about him lately, Henry, the mad man.

A Letter

I have found a poem of ghosts; dead is the muse who inspired it…and dead, is the man who wrote it.

My Victor,

I wrote a serenade, would you like to read it? Well you will despite anything, and it will engrave into your mind and onto those who cross its path as well. If anything, it is my legacy, my tribute to the woman in my life. I promised her I would sing it upon her every presence, dare she fell sick, this poem shall be her remedy. Read it and weep, my friend:

The Canary,

I am an unsentimental man, untouched by the sounds of loon,
And this among the teals, the sparrows and the robins too,
But there was a time within an hour or two,
In which I woke and wept upon the majesty of the moon,

Amidst her sound in the realm of sentiment,

When she had sung her midnight song,
And awoke in me a beating long,
The Canary,

I am an unsentimental man, untouched by the sounds of song,
And well, how can I be anything but,
Since when her wings were torn?
The Canary,

1 December

I am now writing on my way home, for the screeching of this train is piercing and condemns me to this diary. How strange to see all around me move with such a speed yet I myself sit here with a still heart and a deadening breath. My watch has slowed, my home is far away from me, and I cannot rid my mind of this memory. She is staring now, with a smile and a playful glimmer too, how enthusiastic my sweet lover is, hopeful and happy to live my life with me, leaving behind her the soulless city of Kazan and the people of its place. Perhaps I should tell her that I could never forget those people of my past, the kindness of their hearts, and the face of their dead son. Is it fair I bring their voices with us? Oh Isabelle, do you even question what I write on this page? Could you ever imagine it? Well, must I never finish this tragedy? Here is the truth, buried within these pages.

How can I describe that night? It was quiet, for sure. An odd reason had kept me up, so I sat on my bed with no light around me waiting for the red of sun to hue the sky. My room was cold at that time, so I left my bed and intended to close the shutters from the outside world. But there was a light a little below my room, and it was in fact coming from

Alexander's room. I observed through the window for some time; contemplating upon the humanly shadow I could see within, walking about and changing its form from petit to large to monstrous. I was worried and curious, so I took a lantern and left my room. A single light led my way and I was dependent on its exuberance all through the home. Hollow was the air, scented with drawn cigars and aged leather and touched with the slight aroma of the gardens flowers; it was a nice time and very soothing too, despite the mystery that drew me in. I then neared Alexa's room.

The light shimmered from within, and a husky voice too, whispering incomprehension. I looked around for any other but there was no other to notice. So I took it upon myself and I peeked in. with the help of the dim candles I saw victor crouched over the body on the bed, and his pale green robes draped across the floor boards. My friend noticed me; his eyes were red and cheeks moist with tears. Fear designed his face and awoke my own. "My son is dead!" he cried. "Alim, my son…" He looked back onto the boy and placed a hand on his dull skin. I nearly dropped the flame as I ran over to the two. The boy's face was in shock, the gray eyes were awe-struck and the lips twitched with dying life; but he was alive. The shock in me paralyzed my every intention to move. I should have rung Bora, I should have called for Fleur, I should have told Victor his son still breathed. But I just stared at him, miserably. Alexa's panicking hands touched mine, and Victors too, but the father was in delusion, moaning to himself and crying for his "dead son". The lesion on the boy had progressed and now it protruded incredibly and very noticeably too, spilling blood and yellow from its pores. No voice came from Alexa but just the sounds of his retarded breathing. When the frantic moving stopped I found it in myself to grab a small mirror from the pocket of the dissociative father and place it near Alexa's mouth. It was clear, and the boy was dead.

Leading up to the funeral it was I who conducted the formalities. The others were rather unseen to me, hidden within the walls of their home. News spread through the town, condolences were sent and money was given. I once found Kurya weeping solitarily in the formers room; he was oblivious of me, but the sight of him reminded me of my own feelings, for none had I allowed to overcome me. And I believe it is only now I feel the gravity of reality. I tried to speak to the family, but as written, they were hardly seen. When I *had* seen them, it was a strange thing to do so. Blankness and a mysterious visage was expressed from them, and despite my lettered years in reading these things, I was left blind.

The funeral itself went as planned, or however well a planned funeral could carry on. My familiarity with the situation had me become rather obscure to the event. I stood aback and let the others stand in front. Bora had done well to the body; it was clean and innocent, much like the first day I had laid eyes upon its breathing memory. I distracted myself by watching the others through all the time, for a surge rushed through me every time I glanced at the body. Victor stood between Fleur and Audrey, firm, confident and glaring proudly upon the lowering coffin; though I know well the secrets of his heart. Fleur was the unmistakable mother, sobbing persistently and speaking incomprehensively within herself; her future is suspicious to me. And Audrey, the sister, stood with weak limbs. She was considerably distracted by the nature around rather than the matter at hand. I noticed that every time her eyes would lay upon the body, she would grimace and shake her head in a disapproving manner. It was expected, for her last memories with the boy were of disappointing nature. She had grown apart from him, against him almost, and it was at this very moment did she feel the overwhelming regret of it…as I felt the guilt, for a reason I hated not knowing. Isabelle was there too, rather unseen and away from any attention. I watched her for the longest of moments and for the remainder of the ceremony.

A few hours had passed and I sat alone near the gardens. The wind turned cold and the clouds covered the light, and soon the hue of blue too, covering the last remnants of the lighted mood of the day. From my distance I could see Victors lonely figure walk around the grave point for some time, until throwing what it seemed to be a little stone into a nearby pond and walking away out of my sight. Not much later Isabelle came intending to join me at the seat. She said nothing as she sat next to me, nor did I, for I could not find the words that would sound right from my lips. She began to weep, and I placed a hand on hers in what I could see as the only appropriate response. She then said, alarming me, nearly hurting me, "I know, Alim, how you feel about me. As you know how I feel about you." I admit it was hard for me to hear these words, despite how I waited so long for them. She expected my silence, for she continued without anticipating a reply. "It's wrong of me to say this now, at my friend's funeral. I know, but he would have wanted this." I remember shaking my head, all of it, it all sounded so ridiculous to me then. But still she continued speaking, and I listened, slowly coming to realize the reality of who Alexander truly was. "Yes, he would've loved this, my confession to you. We spoke about it so often, and once you almost heard us too." She said with a little laugh. "The way he spoke of you, sometimes I wonder whether it was because of his words did I fall in love with you. Once, before he left for the war again, he asked me about how I felt about you. It's what got me thinking, to be honest, about how I truly felt about you. So I told him, and he…laughed! He already knew, that was him, the way he saw things, he knew so much about the people around him, the people he loved. And he taught me so much about you, Alim. I too asked him whether he knew how you felt about me, considering how close you two were, and he told me of how you did care, about how there was a longing in you, and he noticed that you saw it in me to fulfill it…I know I could never replace the thought of Agata, Alim, but I too feel for you as she loved you, and I want you to understand that. Could you love me the way you loved her?"

How brilliantly did Alexa fool me. How respectfully did he hide his mind from me. I smiled at the moment Isabelle asked her question, an answer she wanted, yet my smile was for the boy; a smile of shame upon his good. How often did he watch me? The moments I caught him staring, was he considering me? Was he reading my heart? The moments he cried to me, I see now that they were beyond my comprehension. I see now, he humored the sessions not for his father, but for me, for my name. My entire time spent here was under the careful care of dear Alexander, who saw through me…as did a younger victor. And how I treated him, dear God, how did I treat him.

Will Isabelle's face be my condemnation? To look her in the eyes, is that my justice? I am trying to face her, yet her exuberance is painful, her laugh is so familiar, her love is painful, nearly daunting to feel. Well, this is my curse now. What a bittersweet thing. We are nearing home. I am forbidding this diary from my eyes, and never shall I look upon it again. Perhaps in time, I may forget and live like Henry.

CPSIA information can be obtained
at www.ICGtesting.com
Printed in the USA
FSOW01n0109140917
38483FS